WELCOME TO JUBILEE

RACHEL HANNA

This book is dedicated to one of my loyal readers, Chris Cox, who came up with the name for this adorable fictional mountain town - Jubilee.

CHAPTER 1

*S*he stared down at her half-eaten chicken salad sandwich. "I don't understand."

"They don't want it, Madeline. I'm so sorry."

Madeline Harper had been one of the world's most successful and famous romance novelists for the last twenty years. Now, sitting across from her agent and friend of almost as many years, she couldn't believe her ears.

"They don't want *any* of it?"

"No, I'm afraid not. The publisher said small town romance is the big thing these days. Your high society, big city romances just aren't selling."

She snorted. "Well, then we'll find another publisher!"

Laura Kearney had been her agent for over fifteen years, and she knew her facial expressions.

This wasn't a good one. In fact, she'd never seen a look on her face like this.

"I've already tried, Madeline. Nobody's interested."

It wasn't like she needed the money desperately. She'd done very well for herself all these years. At only fifty-five years old, she could easily retire and live a nice life off her royalties and savings, but she didn't want to do that. She didn't want to sit somewhere and wither away. She had stories to tell, even if nobody wanted to read them.

"How can this be? I'm a household name in the book world." Maybe her ego was a bit bigger than it needed to be, but it was true. She was known around the world, and now nobody wanted her. They wanted all the younger authors. She'd never felt so washed up in her life.

"You know your last two books didn't do great. I'm afraid the time has come to just go enjoy your life, Madeline. Most writers would kill for the career you've had."

She stared at Laura like she had two heads. "Excuse me? *Had*?"

"I don't want to hurt you, especially after what's happened in your life recently..."

"You think I'm so weak that I can't talk about my

husband leaving me for my best friend? That was over a year ago. I've moved on."

"Have you?"

She hadn't, honestly. She would never forget that morning. As usual, she had a book signing in another city, so she got up, ate breakfast with her husband of twenty-five years, Jacob, and headed out to her Uber. She only got three miles away before realizing she'd left an entire box of books on the dining room table. The Uber driver - she thought his name was Nate - drove her back to the house. As she ran inside, she didn't even notice her best friend Angela's car parked down the street.

She *did* notice her husband kissing her in their living room.

She'd thought they had a pretty good, although slightly stale, marriage. They had a beautiful home with a pool and a gardener. They'd had nice cars and vacations. Although they'd never had children, she thought they would be together forever.

Until that morning.

She didn't like thinking back on it, but being an author made everything play out in her head over and over again like a movie. It was just how her brain worked.

She remembered feeling like her feet were stuck to the floor with industrial strength glue as she watched her husband kiss another woman. Her best friend since middle school. The person she trusted the most in the world, aside from her husband.

There was a lot of screaming and yelling and crying, and then it was over. Her marriage. Her friendship. Her ability to trust people.

Her now ex-husband, Jacob, had also been her manager. He'd read her books and put a second set of eyes on them. He'd organized her book signings. He'd answered emails and letters from readers. Her best friend had always cheered her on, reading every book and handling her social media.

And then one day, she was alone. She had Laura, of course, but everything else had fallen to her. Hiring an assistant had turned out to be a fiasco, so she just did it all herself. Trusting another human wasn't something she was planning to do soon.

"What am I supposed to do now?" she finally asked once she pulled herself out of the memory.

"I don't know, Madeline. If you don't want to retire, maybe try writing something else?"

"Like what?"

Laura contorted her face into a tight ball. "Small town?"

Madeline let out a loud laugh. "Small town? Are you even serious?"

"It's popular!"

"So, what, I'm supposed to write about Farmer Bob and his romance with the town librarian?"

"That's not what a small town is about, Madeline. Maybe you should read a few popular books and see what you think."

"*My* books used to be popular books."

Laura reached across the table and touched her hand. "I know this has to be hard, but sometimes the market changes, and you have to change with it to survive."

"I know nothing about small towns. I grew up right here in Atlanta. The only time I've visited small towns is on book tours, and I got out of there as quickly as I could. I like night life and traffic and restaurants on every corner. How can I write about the boring goings-on in a small town?"

"Well, I do have an idea," she said, barely making eye contact.

Madeline was skeptical. "What kind of idea?"

"My aunt has a rental home in north Georgia, in the Blue Ridge Mountains."

"So?"

"Her tenant moved out, and she's looking to fill it for at least a six-month lease."

"Again, what does this have to do with me?"

"Why don't you rent it?"

"Why would I want to do a thing like that? I'd

rather bang my head against that brick wall over there."

"You can research, Madeline. Learn about small town life. Write a brand new series, and pitch it to publishers."

"You can't be serious."

"I am serious. It's the only way I can think of for you to get a new start. You can't write small town romance without knowing about small towns."

Madeline pondered the thought for a moment. Was she desperate enough to leave her fancy city life behind for a small mountain town?

"Is it some dilapidated cabin in the backwoods near a moonshine still?"

Laura chuckled. "No. My aunt has a lot of money. This place is beautiful. Look." She pulled out her phone and clicked on a picture. The log cabin looked quite large and sat on a beautiful lot with a long-range mountain view. It actually didn't look too bad.

"Would I have neighbors?"

"Just a few. It's a private road."

She liked the sound of that. Although she loved her readers, she didn't want to be approached for auto-graphs all the time. However, the thought of living way back on a private road also gave her the heebie jeebies.

"Alarm system?"

"And cameras. My aunt likes to watch the wildlife while she's away."

"Wildlife?"

Laura laughed. "It's in the mountains, Madeline. There are animals there."

"Like what?" Now, she was getting a little nervous. She loved dogs and even the occasional cat. Aside from that, she preferred animals kept their distance.

"Deer mostly. Some wild turkeys."

"Oh, dear Lord. Wild turkeys? Do they bite?"

"Rarely," Laura said, obviously messing with her.

"What about bears?"

"Occasionally," she said quickly as Madeline's eyes widened. "But they don't like people, and they won't come around as long as you don't put bird feeders in your yard. I heard if you get a larger dog, bears won't come around because of the dog urine in the yard."

Madeline put her face in her hands. "How has my life come to this?"

Laura rubbed her arm. "This is going to be good for you. I truly believe that. You'll come out of this as a better version of yourself."

"Okay, fine. I'll go, but only because I want to prove to those idiot publishers that Madeline Harper can still write great books and compete with the best of them."

"Yay! I'm so excited! I'll text my aunt right now."

"Wait. What's the name of my new hometown?"

Laura smiled. "Jubilee."

AFTER A TWO-HOUR DRIVE, Madeline finally arrived on the edge of Jubilee. After driving over a terrifying, winding mountain road for a good twenty minutes, she felt like she needed to stand on stable ground. She stopped at what appeared to be the town's only red light and looked at her GPS. She still had another fifteen minutes before she'd arrive at the house.

The long drive alone had given her way too much time to think. She wasn't a good relaxer. Other people could sit and meditate. They could be with their thoughts. She wasn't that kind of person. When she wasn't writing, she liked to be busy doing something. Listening to the thoughts rolling through her own brain had never led to anything good, in her opinion.

Instead, she liked to listen to her characters' voices. They were much more entertaining, and she could control them better than her own.

As she drove through the square in the middle of the tiny town of Jubilee, she got her first taste of what life was going to be like there. No skyscrapers. No fancy boutiques. No high end nail salons. Instead, she saw a bookstore, a coffee shop, and the first of many churches.

"This is going to be torture," she said aloud to no one in particular. After all, she was alone in her car. Heck, she was alone in life, too.

There was a part of her that wanted to turn around immediately and head back to the closest big city. She had even lived in suburbs, but they were large, bustling suburbs with all kinds of big box stores. What in the world was she going to do in this godforsaken place? What if she needed a new handbag or a gown to wear to a party?

Instead of stopping to get the coffee that she desperately needed, her curious nature thrust her ever forward toward the cabin that was going to be her home for the next six months. She had second guessed this decision all the way there. She even called Laura one time to beg her to come up with another solution. There was no other solution.

Either she could retire and live off her royalties, or she could try something new. It went against every fiber of her being to change what she was writing just to suit the masses of readers. She had a big fan base, but even they weren't buying her books as frequently as they used to. Maybe she was just washed up. She feared she would write something in the small town genre and still not make it successful.

And then what?

She wouldn't allow herself to think about that question too deeply. It was frightening. At fifty-five years old, starting over with a totally different career - or worse yet, retiring - seemed awful.

All the women in her family had worked until their eighties. It wasn't because they had to, but because they wanted to. She remembered her grandmother retired for a whole two weeks before telling everyone she was losing her mind. She went straight back to work, and she worked until the day she died. That sounded perfect to Madeline.

Her GPS directed her down yet another winding road toward the cabin. As she drove, she saw fewer and fewer houses. She saw a few trailers, a lot of horse farms, and many pastures full of black cows.

She finally heard her GPS tell her to turn right. As she turned, she noticed several mailboxes facing the road, and then she was on a long dirt road. Georgia red clay. It was going to ruin her beautiful white car.

She drove for what seemed like an eternity until she finally came to the address where she would be staying. She stopped in front of the house, in shock at how beautiful the view actually was.

It was a relief to see that she would not be staying in some kind of ramshackle shack that was going to fall in while she was trying to sleep at night. Instead, it was a beautiful log home that looked almost like a lodge you would find in snow-capped mountains out west. Instead, it had a long range view of the Blue Ridge Mountains. She had to admit, it was peaceful.

Maybe a little too peaceful. Suddenly, she started getting visions of an ax murderer coming to take her out while she was sleeping. Who would know? This place was so remote that she felt completely alone in the world. Laura had told her there were neighbors, but she hadn't seen any.

She pulled into the driveway on the side of the house. She sat there for a moment, giving herself one more chance to back out of this whole thing. Maybe she could choose a different career. Interior designer? Real estate agent? No. She was a writer, and she always would be.

She stepped out of the car and walked to the back to retrieve her overnight bag. The rest of her things that she would need for the next six months were being shipped to her. For now, she had what she needed. Of course, she would have to go to the grocery store immediately because there was no food in the house.

She walked up the three steps to the front porch. The porch was wide, enough for four or five people to stand shoulder to shoulder. There was a wooden swing suspended from the ceiling above. The house had a porch wrapping around three sides of it, and there was a gazebo built in between two of the decks.

Madeline decided she would come out and investigate the rest of the property once she got settled in. She wanted to see where she would sleep and eat for the next few months.

As she turned the lock on the door and opened it, she was surprised at how beautiful it was inside. Laura had told her the truth. It was apparent that her aunt had a lot of money and didn't skimp when it came to furnishing the place. The living room had twenty-five foot ceilings, at least. There were beams crossing overhead and a beautiful wall of windows overlooking the back porch and the mountain view. She could only imagine what it looked like at sunrise and sunset.

There was a beautiful stone fireplace, a dining area and an open kitchen with a breakfast bar and granite countertops. No longer did she have to fear that she was going to be cooking on a camp stove in the middle of a house where the floors were falling in. That was the problem with being an author - a very overactive imagination.

She set her bag down on the sofa. Thankfully, the place was furnished or she would've had a really hard time living there. It seemed that Laura's aunt had excellent taste. The overstuffed light brown sofas in the living room really went well with the light colored hardwood floors.

She slowly walked around. There was a guest room on the main level along with a large bathroom and laundry room. Her bedroom was the only one upstairs, and it had a loft attached to it where she could look down at the living room. She had her own bathroom with a corner jetted tub and a separate shower, a large walk-in closet, and a balcony off her bedroom that again gave her a beautiful view of the mountains.

There was also a basement, and she would go down there later. Laura told her it had another bedroom, bathroom, bar, and a pool table. Of course, there was also a living room with a TV where one could watch movies and such.

She allowed her shoulders to descend from her ears, where they had been stuck ever since she had agreed to doing this. At least the place she was going to be living was actually livable. In fact, it was pretty nice. Although, her biggest fear right now was being out in the woods alone. That was something she had never done. Her idea of camping included a hotel and room service.

As Madeline walked through the kitchen, she noticed a can of bear spray sitting on the counter. That didn't bode well. There was also a note telling her where to find the golf cart key. She would need that to drive down and get her mail every day. Was she supposed to take the bear spray with her to get her mail? Was she risking her life just to pick up some free coupons and insurance offers?

She walked back outside onto the porch overlooking the mountains and closed her eyes, taking in a deep breath of mountain air. She had to admit, it felt cleaner. There were no sounds except for birds. It was almost surreal. When was the last time she heard quiet? Can you actually hear quiet?

Her stomach rumbled and broke the quiet. She needed food in the house, and what better way to see her new town than go grocery shopping?

CHAPTER 2

*A*fter two wrong turns while trying to find her way back to the downtown area of Jubilee, Madeline finally located the grocery store. It wasn't what she'd been expecting.

Instead of some large, big box store like she had on every corner back in the city, there was one grocery store in Jubilee. It was called Maynard's. The name even sounded country.

The place looked like it had been open since God was a boy, but she could see on the sign that it had been there since nineteen-fifty-one. The grocery store was old enough to have grandchildren… and maybe great-grandchildren.

She parked her car in one of the few parking spots and started walking toward the door of the small brick building. Before she could make it to the cart corral, an orange cat rubbed against her leg.

"What on earth?" she yelled, practically jumping out of her skin.

"Oh, that's just Larry, one of the colony." She turned to see a young woman walking up behind her. She had a bright blue apron on with a name tag that said Serena.

"Colony?"

"We have a bunch of feral cats that live over by the dumpster."

Madeline turned her head and noticed three more cats at the end of the building.

"Shouldn't someone call animal control?"

Serena chuckled. "You're not from around here, are you?"

Madeline cleared her throat and considered jumping for joy that she wasn't from this place where feral cats roamed free and there were no big box stores. Who wanted to be from here?

"No, I'm not."

"We don't have strict restrictions about where animals can roam up here. After all, they were here first." Serena pushed two carts into the corral.

"But who takes care of them? Gets them their shots and so forth?"

Serena looked at Madeline like she was from

another planet. "Nobody gives shots to feral cats. And we feed them. They like living here. They get meat scraps and cat food. Look at Willie over there. He's fat as a hog!"

Madeline turned to see a fluffy white cat who looked like he'd been rolling in dirt. She had to admit he didn't look like he was wasting away.

Without another word, Madeline pushed her cart through the front door and was immediately taken aback. The place was smaller than any grocery store she'd ever been to. It was similar in size to most convenience stores, but set up like a normal grocery store with sections like produce, meat, and dairy.

The place smelled older, and she thought for a moment about turning around and going back to her car. Of course, what would she eat? Maybe she could grow her own food at the cabin. She quickly wiped that thought from her brain since she was about as far from having a green thumb as one of the feral cats outside.

"Excuse me?" Madeline said, walking over to the woman standing behind the only cash register. She looked to be in her seventies, at least, and the years hadn't been kind to her.

"Yeah?" the woman said, her voice coarse. She definitely wasn't the friendly sort, and she was eyeing Madeline like she was there to rob the place.

"Do you offer grocery delivery?"

"Grocery delivery?" the woman, whose name tag said Juanita, stared at her.

"Yes. Like Instacart?"

"Insta what?"

Madeline could tell this was going nowhere fast. "Never mind."

She rolled her cart toward the produce section and was surprised to see so many options. They had iceberg and Romaine lettuce, several kinds of tomatoes, and lots of fresh Vidalia onions. She began filling her cart with the fresh fruit and vegetables, relieved that she wouldn't be forced to eat Vienna sausages from a can for dinner.

Madeline finished choosing her produce and turned to go to one of the center aisles to get some staples like sugar and flour. The aisles were quite narrow, and she noticed two women standing in the middle of this one, their carts pulled together. Not wanting to interrupt, she stayed at one end and pretended to look at cereal for an extended period of time.

"Well, you know Marla is divorcing Harold, don't you?" one woman said. She was tall, thin, and had the reddest hair Madeline had ever seen. It was straight out of a box, of course, because God didn't make hair that color.

The other woman gasped. "What? Isn't he a deacon at the church? The pastor won't look kindly on that."

"Esther told Helen that Marla met a new man two towns over, and she'd been carrying on a sordid love affair with him for over a year!" The woman was whispering loudly so anyone could hear her.

Madeline had to admit she found the whole thing entertaining. Being an author lent itself well to enjoy gossip, even when she didn't know the people involved.

"How's your mama doing? Is her gout still acting up?"

"Excuse me," Madeline finally said, not wanting to hear about anyone's gout issues.

The women looked at her for a long moment and then slowly pulled their carts back enough for her to get by.

"Some people are so rude. She must not be from around here," the red-headed woman whispered to the other woman. Madeline chose to ignore it.

She rolled her cart to the next aisle and perused the canned goods.

Living up on the mountain meant she needed to stock up more than she would have back in the city. She loved making soups and chili when she had the time, so she loaded the cart with canned tomatoes and beans. She walked down farther to get some canned fruit because she liked to put mandarin oranges in her salad. She wondered for a moment if people around here even knew what mandarin oranges were.

Maybe she was being too judgmental, but she was also exhausted after her drive. She just wanted to get back to the house and settle in for the night. She could think about the new book she needed to write tomorrow. What she needed right now was a good eight hours of sleep.

As she drove up the gravel road toward the house, Madeline looked around at her neighbors' houses. First, there was what appeared to be a small farm on the corner of her road and the main road. She could see a red barn and a small log home, along with some fenced areas for animals, although she didn't see any animals.

Then, a little further down, there was another log cabin on the left with a long driveway. Nobody was outside, so she didn't know who lived there. After a third of a mile, she arrived at her house. Well, her temporary house. She doubted she would ever refer to Jubilee as home.

In her books, she often wrote about "fish out of water" characters who had a hard time fitting into new situations. Now, she knew what those characters felt like. Having grown up in Atlanta and lived there her whole life, Jubilee felt like a foreign country. She almost felt as if she needed to learn a new language and the customs of the area.

The one thing she was happy about was the remoteness of the house. Nobody would bother her out here. She could just write in peace and spend time alone, something she enjoyed.

Years ago, her life was so different. She was always traveling with her husband, going from book signing to book signing. She had huge events where she spoke to dozens of readers at a time. But in the past few years, that had waned. The invitations had slowed way down, and she had to admit it had shaken her confidence a bit.

Confidence was something Madeline had never lacked. Even as a kid, she was talented at most of the things she tried. Tennis, soccer, writing. She was used to getting compliments on her looks and her talents. She always wore designer clothing and dressed like she was prepared for any social event. These days, compliments were few and far between. Aging was hard.

Sometimes she looked in the mirror and didn't

know who was looking back. That formerly beautiful young woman was transforming before her eyes. Crow's feet, forehead wrinkles, those little lines around her lips. She'd thought about going to the dermatologist to "touch up" her face, but after seeing what some of those procedures had done to her wealthy friends in the city, she was still too scared to try it. She didn't want to come out looking like she'd gone through a wind tunnel.

She parked her car in the driveway and opened the door. Before her foot even hit the ground, she heard a voice.

"Hey there! Let me help you get those groceries inside." A woman, who looked to be in her seventies, was standing right beside her car. Where had she come from?

"Excuse me?"

"I'm Geneva Whitby. I live down the road." She pointed past the house, to the other end of the gravel road. Madeline hadn't driven down that far yet.

"Nice to meet you. I don't need any help, though. Thanks for the offer." Madeline stepped out and opened her trunk. Geneva grabbed a grocery bag and started walking toward Madeline's front door.

"It's no bother, really."

She was spry for an older woman. She had curly gray hair with flecks of black. It was a wild mane of

hair that looked like it hadn't been brushed today…
or yesterday. She was wearing a colorful dress that
almost dragged the ground, and she had red cat-eye
glasses.

Madeline picked up the other two bags and
closed the trunk. By the time she looked up, Geneva
was already standing at Madeline's front door.

"You really didn't have to help me. I could've
gotten these on my own," Madeline said, trying not
to sound rude but feeling a little violated.

"Honey, that's just what we do around here. We
help each other survive in this wild place."

Wild place? That sounded a bit ominous. She
chose to believe living in the woods of the Blue
Ridge Mountains was no different from living in her
spacious home back in the city. If she thought too
hard about what was in those woods around her, she
might never leave the house.

They walked inside, and Geneva headed straight
for the kitchen like she lived there. She'd obviously
been in the house before, and Madeline wondered if
maybe she did this to every renter.

"Thanks for the help…" Madeline said, cutting
her eyes toward the door in an effort to lead her
back outside. Ignoring Madeline's hint, Geneva
walked to the wall of windows across from the
kitchen.

"Boy, you sure do have a beautiful view here. My cabin is down in the woods, so I don't get much of a view."

"Sorry to hear that." Madeline waited for the woman to walk to the front door, but instead she sat down at the kitchen table. She was beginning to feel like this might be the worst day of her life.

"So, what brings you to Jubilee?" she asked, smiling expectantly.

Madeline cleared her throat. "Just an extended vacation."

Geneva eyed her carefully. "You don't want to tell me, do you?"

"I just did."

She chuckled. "It's all right. You don't have to tell me."

Was this woman a mind reader? Maybe she did tarot cards and had a crystal ball in her woodsy little cabin.

"It's getting late, and I need to start dinner."

Geneva smiled. "I'll bring you some of my home-made Brunswick Stew. I do a lot of canning, so I have plenty. You can have it on hand for nights like this when you're too tired to cook. I'll drop it off tomorrow." She walked toward the door.

"You really don't have to do that."

She waved her hand and kept walking. "It's no problem. Have a good night!"

And just like that, Geneva was gone from her house, and Madeline locked the door. Suddenly, she heard the knob jiggling and turned to see Geneva standing there on the other side of the glass.

Madeline opened the door.

"Why is your door locked?"

She stared at her. "For safety?"

Geneva let out a loud laugh. "Honey, nobody locks their doors around here!"

"Well, I do. Now, what can I help you with?"

"I was just going to say that if you need anything, here's my phone number. I wrote it on a card for you before I walked over here, but I forgot to give it to you."

Madeline accepted it, if for no other reason than to get this woman to go home. "Thanks."

This time, she watched Geneva walk down the gravel road toward her house, just to make sure she was gone for good.

AFTER COOKING a basic meal of baked chicken and a sweet potato, Madeline had crashed. The long day of travel and the stress of trying to make her way around a new town had left her frazzled and spent. She wasn't normally a late sleeper, but this morning she was surprised when she opened her eyes and saw that it was almost eight-thirty.

For most of her career, she'd woken up at six, had her first cup of strong coffee, and started writing her words for the day. She would break for lunch and have her typical Cobb salad with no croutons and then go back to writing.

Structure was her greatest ally. While many writers only wrote when creativity struck, she wrote day in and day out like clockwork. Sure, sometimes she didn't feel particularly inspired to write, but she did it anyway. That often meant going back later and cleaning up those same words.

She sat on the side of the bed for a moment and surveyed her new surroundings. The bed was made of rustic, rough-hewn logs, and the walls and ceiling of the room were made of polished wood. It felt a bit like she'd slept in a treehouse.

Madeline stood up and opened the blinds leading out onto the deck off her bedroom. It was a sunny day, not a cloud in the blue sky. She opened the door and stepped out onto the porch in her pajamas, which consisted of a matching set with a top and shorts. There were little books on them, a gift her husband gave her last year. Now she felt like burning them, but they were too cute.

As she stared out over the blue tinged mountains, she finally took a deep breath. The last few weeks had been challenging, to say the least. Losing her marriage and watching her business implode at the same time hadn't been easy. Most people would've cried by now, but not Madeline. She didn't cry. It wasn't in her nature. She considered herself a strong woman, and in her mind strong women didn't cry.

Of course, her characters cried all the time. She learned early in her career that she had to make them cry or readers got upset. In one of her earliest books, a woman's husband died, and Madeline never made her cry. She got so many letters about how unrealistic it was. Her editor had tried to tell her, but Madeline was stubborn to a fault. When her readers told her something, however, she tended to listen since they paid her bills.

This morning, she didn't have time to dillydally around. She had to write. After all, the whole purpose of being in Jubilee was to write a new book so she could prove to her publishers that she wasn't some washed up, middle-aged author who couldn't move with the times.

Well, she guessed she wasn't even middle-aged anymore. At fifty-five years old, she would have to live to be one-hundred ten for that to be true. Aging was a blessing, but it was also mentally difficult at times. Realizing that half of her life was already over was something she didn't like to think about. Madeline wasn't great at relaxation or sitting around thinking about things. She had a go-getter type of personality, and that rarely lent itself well to writing deep, emotional books.

Still, she had created a very successful career. It was only recently that she learned that the landscape was changing, and she could be old news very quickly. She didn't like to admit to herself that the emails raving about her books had slowed down quite a bit in recent years. She didn't get as much fan mail anymore, and the invitations to book signings were drying up, as well.

In that way, getting older stunk.

Her agent tried to convince her that it had nothing to do with her age, and a lot more to do with her not keeping up with the times. She didn't like to write trends. She didn't want to change what she wrote just because readers were looking for something else. But it was important because if readers didn't want to buy her books, there was no reason for her to write. At this point, she had no choice but to change directions to keep up with the times and have some hope of saving her career.

Now that she was single, she needed income. She needed something to keep her busy. The thought of her ever dating again was horrifying. Who wanted to date at her age? What was she supposed to do? Get on one of those trendy new dating apps? No, thank you. She had no interest in meeting men on the Internet. She had seen enough true-crime documentaries to know that rarely ended well.

She walked back into the bedroom and quickly changed into her comfortable writing outfit. She always wore the same sort of thing when she wrote - yoga pants, a loose-fitting T-shirt, and her favorite black flats. She had to be comfortable when she wrote, or else she got annoyed and the words wouldn't flow.

Madeline put on a pot of coffee and set up a space to write at the kitchen table. She had other areas in the house where she could sit at a desk, but she wanted to look out over the mountain view to give her some inspiration. At some point she'd have to go into town and actually interact with the locals to make sure that her book was realistic. For now, she just needed to get started. She needed to feel the words flow out of her fingers and onto the digital page.

The coffee finished brewing, and she added the requisite amounts of cream and sugar before sitting

down at the table in front of her laptop. This felt like
some kind of new beginning. Not one that she had
asked for, but a new beginning nonetheless. She
closed her eyes and took a deep breath, blowing it
out of her mouth before putting her fingers over the
keys.

Just as she was about to type the first words of
her new novel, she heard a ruckus outside unlike
anything she had ever heard before. She didn't know
what it was, but it sounded like war. She ran to the
window to look out, but she couldn't see anything.
Stupidly, she opened the front door and poked her
head out, trying to figure out what direction it was
coming from. Each time there was a loud noise, like
a gunshot, and then she would hear what sounded
like rain falling from the trees. Then, birds would fly
the other direction. This definitely did not seem
normal.

Aggravated at the interruption in her workday,
she grabbed the key to the golf cart and decided to
investigate. It was probably a stupid thing to do,
given that she had no idea where she was going or
who she might encounter. But if this was how things
were going to be every day while she was trying to
work, she had to nip it in the bud right now.

There was one thing that Madeline would say
about herself – she wasn't typically scared of things.

Living in the city had given her a thick skin when it came to dealing with other people. She had no filter between her brain and her mouth, and she could easily say the wrong thing to someone. Running on adrenaline, she hopped on the golf cart and backed out of the driveway onto the gravel road. As she drove, she heard another shot, followed by the sound of what seemed to be small pebbles falling from the trees. Again, she couldn't see anything.

When she heard the next shot, she knew she was getting closer to the source. Hopefully, this would not be the beginning of her obituary. *"Noted romance novelist, Madeline Harper, was killed today out in the middle of the woods when she drove toward gunshots like an absolute idiot."*

Finally, she arrived at the location in question. She saw a man off in the distance in the middle of a field, pointing what appeared to be some kind of rifle toward the sky. Was this guy really trying to shoot birds as they were flying over? Or was he crazy and thought he was shooting at some sort of alien spacecraft?

She jumped out of the golf cart and stomped over to the fence that separated his property from the gravel road. "Excuse me! Excuse me!" she yelled toward him. He was wearing some sort of head-phones, so he removed them and dropped them onto the ground before setting his gun on the ground as well. Thank God he did that because she was afraid he was going to approach her with that in his hand.

"Can I help you?" he asked as he walked toward her. The closer he got, the more she could tell about him. He was wearing a pair of well-worn jeans, cowboy boots that looked like they had seen better days, and a tight fitting grayish blue T-shirt. He was muscular, to say the least. He was tall. He had on a baseball cap, although she bet he wore cowboy hats a lot of the time. He looked about her age, maybe a little younger. Dark brown hair with little hints of blonde in it. And then there was the smile. That lazy, southern smile. She was feeling butterflies in her stomach, and that annoyed the heck out of her.

"What on earth are you doing out here? It's very noisy, and it's early in the morning."

He walked closer until he was a few feet away and leaned one shoulder against a tree. "It's called skeet shooting. You've never heard of it?"

Of course she had heard of skeet shooting. For some reason, the thought had not entered her mind. "I'm not an idiot. I've heard of skeet shooting."

He slowly nodded his head, slightly smiling as if he was amused by her presence. "We do a lot of that around here."

"Well, I'm trying to work. It would be really great

if it didn't sound like Rambo was in the woods beside my house every time I'm trying to get my work done."

"Noted. I'm sorry I interrupted your morning, ma'am." He tipped his baseball cap in her direction.

"Don't call me ma'am. I'm not that old."

"I'm Brady Nolan," he said, reaching his hand out toward hers. She stared at it for a moment and finally put her hand in his. It was warm and large. It was rough. It was nice.

"Madeline Harper."

"Nice to meet you. So I assume you're my new neighbor?"

"Just for a few months. I'm working on a project."

"Oh, I've heard that before."

"You've heard that people work on projects before?" she said, sarcastically.

"No, I've heard people say they won't be staying up here in these mountains for very long. Few people make it out."

She crossed her arms. "That sounds ominous."

Brady laughed. "Nothing ominous. It's just that these mountains will take a hold of you if you're not careful. I don't know of another place on earth I'd rather live."

She laughed under her breath. "I can think of at least five places off the top of my head."

"Sorry to disturb you this morning," he said, tipping his baseball cap her direction again before turning to walk away. Madeline stood there for a moment, unsure of what to say or do since the man seemed to have just stopped their conversation. It wasn't that she wanted to continue talking to him, but it seemed kind of rude.

She turned and walked back to the golf cart, climbed in and looked over at him one more time. He picked up his gun and started walking back toward the barn. She sat there for a moment, watching him go inside.

As she drove back toward the cabin, she wondered how she was going to survive in this crazy place. There was so much that she wasn't used to, starting with the good-looking cowboy that lived on the corner of her road.

CHAPTER 3

$\mathcal{M}$adeline returned to the cabin and decided to sit outside to do her writing. Maybe the beautiful surroundings would inspire her. She grabbed her notepad and sat down in one of the four rocking chairs on the back deck, overlooking the Blue Ridge Mountains. She was still one of those old souls who often wrote their books on notepads. She used a combination of tactics when it came to writing books. Sometimes she hand wrote them, and sometimes she typed. Either way, all the words ended up in her computer before it was over.

It was a beautiful early spring morning, still a bit cool outside, still some dew on the grass. The lovely view was a stark contrast to all the tumultuous thoughts that were running through her mind. After she'd had the heated exchange with her new, strikingly handsome neighbor, she wasn't feeling exactly peaceful. She reached over and picked up her coffee mug, one of her favorites with a book quote on it, and took a long sip.

The sound of the silence in the mountains was almost deafening, especially for someone who was used to the city. The honking horns, the constant white noise of people talking… and sometimes screaming. The hum of traffic, the shriek of sirens. None of that was here. All she could hear were birds. She'd never realized how many bird sounds there were until she was away from the city.

The more she listened, the more she heard. The rustling of leaves, the wind blowing through the trees, the distant bark of a dog, and maybe even the faint echo of a gunshot. Was her neighbor still shooting skeet? Had he not learned his lesson?

She looked down at the empty paper again, placing her pen against it. Small-town life. This is what she was supposed to write about. How in the world was she going to create something interesting around such a dull topic? Nothing happened here. Or at least it seemed that way. There were just a bunch of smiling people going about their day when she drove through town. After all, didn't people come here for a quiet life? How was she supposed to create something compelling in a setting like this?

Madeline had never been good at relaxation. Long ago, she had given up meditation and yoga because her mind never stopped. She would always think of some great book idea right in the middle of a meditation session and run to her desk to write it down. Even when she would go to the beach with friends in her younger years, they would all be laying out in the sun trying to get a tan while she was frantically looking for the best seashells on the beach. She just wasn't somebody who enjoyed relaxing. And this place she was living now? It was like one big meditation.

She would have to rely on her skills. They had held her in good stead her entire life. She was known for her beautiful prose and her talent for character descriptions that were so vivid; the people seemed to be real. She could describe the city with her eyes closed, using one million different adjectives. She had always relied on her own personal experiences and observations, but she had none for this place or these people.

Laura's words echoed in her head. "You need to live in a small town and learn about the people." She had reiterated this to Madeline time and time again, but right now she was finding it very hard to even come up with one sentence about this place.

Madeline looked down at her watch and realized

almost an hour had passed, and she still had no words on the page. She had spent the whole morning brooding and pouting rather than writing. If she was going to make the most out of this six-month period, and maybe even go home early, she was going to have to get words on the paper.

"Jubilee. A quaint little town nestled in the Blue Ridge Mountains…." She grumbled to herself. These words were not good enough. They were not the words of noted novelist Madeline Harper. She was phoning it in, and that wouldn't do.

Again, she found herself distracted by all the sounds of the forest. There was a horse neighing in the distance, and she could hear what sounded like a tractor's engine off in the distance. And was that a gun shot again?

She put her pad of paper and pen on the table next to her and sighed. This was exasperating. If she craned her head, she could see Brady down at his farm working on something. The trees had not regained all of their leaves yet, but she imagined when they did she wouldn't be able to see a thing other than her own home. Her neighbors weren't exactly close.

She had to understand this place better if she was going to write about it. She gathered up her resolve and picked up her pen, but this time not to write;

instead she needed to make a list of what she needed to do to research this small town. She had to get to know Jubilee, the people who lived there, and what they loved about it. Maybe she would even ask Brady some questions since he seemed to be a native.

Madeline laughed under her breath as she stood up to walk back into the house and change her clothes. Her readers would probably have a good chuckle right now if they knew where she was and what she was planning. She wasn't even sure this was possible. But the only way to do it would be to go into town and start getting an idea of how this place really worked.

IT WAS early spring in the mountains which meant that it was still quite cool outside. Madeline wrapped herself in a lightweight shawl and she stepped out onto the porch before turning around to lock the door. In the city, you always locked your doors. She didn't care what Geneva said.

The sun was starting to peek over the mountain tops, casting long shadows across the yard. She could hear the squawking of crows, and it sounded like they outnumbered the people. As she walked to her car, ready to drive into the city and start checking it out, she saw two deer standing in the bottom of the yard, the mountains providing a beautiful backdrop to the scene. That was something she never saw in the city – deer. Long ago, progress had wiped away their home. She stood for a moment, watching them as they watched her. They didn't seem particularly scared, but she was pretty sure if she moved toward them, they would run away.

She got into her car and backed out of the driveway, deciding that she would spend as many hours as she could delving into the heart of Jubilee. The only way to write a good book was to do your research. And that was true in this case, even if she just wanted to get in her car and go back home. Not to the cabin, but to the city.

Madeline was an author who didn't experience writer's block regularly, so this was exhausting and painful for her. There were moments where she thought maybe she wasn't cut out for this anymore. Maybe she was getting too old and should hand over the world of publishing to the younger ones. But then she was also stubborn. Very stubborn. And there was no way she was going to walk away from the thing she loved most in the world.

Writing had always been her companion. From

the youngest age, she wrote. She kept journals in school, wrote poetry, wrote stories. People thought she was weird in middle school, and she got bullied for being a "nerd", but that didn't stop Madeline. Stubbornness had helped her even back in those days. As much as she loved writing, she found herself sometimes loving it too much. Loving it more than people.

There was a moment after her divorce when she realized that she had loved writing more than her husband. And that made her feel really bad about herself. What kind of person felt that way? But she was an honest person, even when it was painful to think about. There was a good chance she would spend the rest of her life alone because there was no way she was going to get into a relationship with anyone she didn't love again.

She had gotten married all those years ago because she felt like that was what was expected of her. After all, who would want to read the books of a romance novelist who didn't have any romance in her life? It wasn't that she didn't care about Jacob, her ex-husband, but she hadn't been desperately in love with him like the characters she wrote about in her books. Sometimes, she would be writing a character and feeling jealous about the romance they had in their lives. It was silly, since they were fictional and completely made up in her own mind, but feelings are feelings.

She drove down the gravel road, unable to keep herself from glancing over at Brady's little farm. She couldn't tell exactly what he did there. Maybe she would ask and put it into her book. She turned left to head towards town, starting down the series of winding roads that would lead her there. Everywhere she looked, there was farmland, rolling green hills full of cows and the occasional donkey. Just as she was turning one of the corners, she stopped dead in her tracks because there was a traffic jam.

She was used to traffic jams back in the city, but they were a bit different from this one because this one had no cars. It was all cows. A giant herd of cows.

Annoyed, she honked her horn, but the cows just looked at her like she was the crazy one. Like they were supposed to be in the middle of the road while she was trying to get somewhere, and she was the invader.

She rolled her window down and hung her head out the window. "Get out of the way! Get out of the way!" She continued honking her horn until finally one of the cows started to slowly walk across the road. Apparently she was the leader, because the other cows started to follow her, several of them giving her the side eye like she was really inter-rupting their day.

As she waited for them to finish crossing the road, an older man appeared next to her window, just across the street. "You okay, ma'am?" he called to her.

"I will be once these stupid cows get out of the road. That's a hazard!"

The old man chuckled a bit at her reaction. "It's pretty common around these parts. You must not be from around here."

"I'm not," she said, forcing a smile. What she wanted to say was "thank goodness I am not from this godforsaken place." But she thought better of it.

"Well, welcome to Jubilee." He continued walking back down his driveway toward his home where he had been getting the mail. By the time Madeline looked back at the road, the cows were finally out of the road and she could continue her drive into the town square.

It took her about fifteen minutes, but when she finally arrived, it was very easy to find a parking place. Of course, it was the middle of the week, and she wondered if the weekends were busier. Did people come down from the mountains to do their shopping? Was there any tourism here? These were all questions she would get the answer to at some point, but for now she needed to figure out where to go first.

The first place she decided to stop was the coffee shop. The place, aptly named Perky's, seemed quite busy for such a small town. Housed in a historic building, the smell of the freshly brewed coffee and homemade pastry hung in the air as she walked in the door. Coffee shops pretty much all smelled the same, which gave her a comforting feeling like she was back in her favorite one in the city. But the similarities really ended there. This place was pretty large, with a fireplace right in the center. There was what appeared to be a community room with the door closed on one side, but the rest of the coffee shop was open.

There was an area where people could play board games or do puzzles. There were tables and chairs, but there were also sofas and overstuffed armchairs scattered about. Of course, there was the requisite long bar where you ordered and then picked up your coffee on the end. She could hear the background chatter of everyone sitting at the tables, talking with friends. There was laughter, hints of gossip, people waving at her and saying hello.

It wasn't that people were unfriendly in the city, but they weren't this level of friendly. The south in general was a friendly place, but this small town was way more than she was counting on. Everybody smiled and waved. People spoke to her. She wasn't a fan of it.

The sound of coffee cups clattering about and the hissing of the espresso machine helped to drown out the need for conversation. Everybody seemed to know everybody by name. People were hugging like they hadn't seen each other in ten years. All of it felt very odd to her.

She walked over to the barista, who had a smile as big as the town square, and looked at the board to figure out what to order. All the coffees had cute little mountain names, and she wasn't sure if she could bring herself to say them.

"Welcome to Perky's. I'm Haley. Are you new to town?"

Madeline stared at her for a moment. "I am. Just visiting."

"Well, we're glad to have you! What can I get for you?" Her twangy, high-pitched voice was a little much for this early in the day.

"Normally I like to get a white chocolate mocha latte at my coffee shop back in the city. What would be the equivalent of that here?"

Haley scratched her nose and then turned around and looked at the big sign behind her. "I'm thinking the Bigfoot Bomber might be your best bet."

Madeline cleared her throat. "Great. Then I'll take a medium Bigfoot Bomber," she said, the words hanging in her mouth.

"We'll get that ready for you," Haley said, taking her credit card. She handed it back and smiled again. "Can I get your name?"

For a moment, Madeline was a bit taken aback. Normally, people would recognize her. After all, she had been a famous romance novelist for decades. She had been on TV, in newspapers and magazines. She did book signings all over the world. But this was a young woman who probably wasn't in her demographic.

"Madeline."

She grinned. "That's a pretty name. We'll call you when it's ready, Madeline."

Madeline walked over and found a table in the corner, hoping to stay away from curious onlookers. She remembered when she was a kid, her grand-mother dragged her to the little southern Baptist church that she went to. Madeline didn't want to go to Sunday school where she wouldn't know the kids, so she stayed in "big church" with her grandmother. As soon as she walked in the door, people descended, shaking her little hand and welcoming her. And it always confused her how they knew she was new there. She liked to blend into the crowd and speak on her own terms if she wanted to. But for some reason these people immediately knew that she was not a regular visitor, and that was the feeling she was getting here.

The table she chose gave her a good vantage point to observe everything going on in the coffee shop. She pretended to look down at her phone as she waited for her coffee so that people didn't think she was staring at them. She was immediately drawn to a group of women sitting around a large table with their heads bent over working on what appeared to be a large quilt. She could hear the hum of their conversation as their laughter filled the coffee shop. It was easy to see that these women were good friends.

She watched as their fingers moved with ease, obviously skilled and practiced. They stitched together the patches of fabric as they chatted and laughed, telling stories and giving advice. She had often wished that she had some kind of creative talent other than writing. One summer, between book deadlines, she decided to try to learn to knit. That did not go well. She also tried watercolor painting until her teacher told her there was no hope. She had but one talent, as far as she was concerned, and that was writing. Maybe that was why she was trying so hard to save it. The days of being good at everything were long gone, left behind in her childhood. It was harder to learn new things as an adult.

She turned her attention back to the women, watching the quilting circle that she had only heard about maybe once or twice in her life. This sort of thing didn't go on in the big city coffee shops. They were much too busy and packed with people coming in and out, hurrying to their jobs. One thing she had already noticed about Jubilee was how much slower paced it was. It was like nobody had anywhere to go, and they took their time with everything they did.

As she watched them continue to put the quilt together, she thought about how each piece of fabric was different than the other. How each probably told a story or maybe came from somewhere special. Maybe old pieces of clothing from loved ones gone. She didn't know the purpose of the quilt or what they were doing with it, but she knew that even the act of putting it together was much like what she did to put together a story. She got out her notepad and started jotting things down, feeling a little spark of inspiration that hadn't been there previously.

"Madeline!" a young man called from behind the counter, holding up her cup of coffee as he smiled. She walked over and took it from him.

"Thanks." She turned quickly and went back to

her table, not wanting anyone to hear her name
called. It would've probably been smarter to use a
fake name, but she wasn't sure if she could keep that
up. The last thing she needed was a crowd of fans
coming to ask for her autograph while she was
trying to research for her next book. To her surprise,
when she looked around the coffee shop, nobody
was really paying attention to her name being called.
Nobody was rushing over. Feeling relieved and a
little disappointed at the same time, she went back
to observing the quilting circle.

Just as she was getting deep into her writing, a
shadow appeared over her paper. She looked up to
see an older woman standing there, holding a piece
of fabric and smiling. "I'm sorry to bother you," she
said, her southern drawl deep. "You wouldn't happen
to be Madeline Harper, would you?"

Madeline smiled. "I am, actually. I'm just visiting
Jubilee for a bit."

The older woman grinned from ear to ear. "It's
very nice to meet you. I hope you're enjoying Jubilee
so far?"

Madeline nodded. "Certainly. It's a nice little
town." A part of her felt comfortable finally getting
noticed.

"Dahlia has a beautiful home, doesn't she?"
"Dahlia?"

"Oh, that's right. You know her niece, Laura, don't you?"

Madeline suddenly realized that Dahlia was the owner of the cabin, and that this woman hadn't recognized her at all. "Right."

"Dahlia and I went to high school together. I was sad when she moved away, but I guess the beach was calling her name. She phoned and told me you'd be staying at her home for a few months. I do hope you enjoy your visit here. Dahlia said you write poetry?"

"Actually novels."

"Oh, I see. Well, I hope you do well with whatever you write."

The woman, a mop of gray hair sitting on top of her head, held a piece of patchwork across her arms. The bright colors clashed with the pale pink cardigan she was wearing. "That's beautiful. I've never seen a quilting circle before. I've heard about them, but I hadn't seen one in person."

"Oh, really? A group of us have been doing this for years. Each of the pieces of fabric have a story, and sometimes we make them for grieving widows whose husbands have died. We take pieces of their old shirts and create a quilt. The one we're making now is actually for a young mother who lost her daughter. We're using some of her baby clothes and dresses from when she was in school to make a quilt in memory of her."

Madeline's eyes threatened to water. She'd never really thought about how meaningful a quilt like that could be for someone. "That's a very kind thing to do."

"Up here in the mountains, we are storytellers, much like you. We just tell our tales in a different way. Through sewing, through cooking, through music, through stories handed down from generation to generation."

"That's a beautiful way to look at it."

"In fact, Jubilee is very much like this quilt. All of our different stories, our different lives, sewn together, but creating a wonderfully colorful community."

"I'll be here for six months, so I hope to get to know more about the town and its people. It will help me write my book. By the way, what's your name?"

"My name is Ruby Sutton."

"Well, it was very nice to meet you, Ruby." Madeline watched as she walked back over to the quilting circle, no doubt to spread the news that she was in town. She fully expected several of the other women to come over to meet her as she returned to her notepad, her pen dancing across the paper as she wrote down some thoughts after the interaction. Surprisingly, when she looked up, nobody was paying attention to her. No one else came over to talk to her. Maybe Ruby didn't tell them who she was.

For a brief moment in time, writer's block dissipated, and Madeline was able to start putting words on the paper. Sitting in town, seeing all the activity around her, she was able to feel more creative. Although the view from her new home was beautiful, it didn't exactly inspire the characters she needed for her new novel. The town had a personality of its own, much like any town, and she had to tap into that. There were people that would become characters, and she just had to find them.

After finishing her drink, Madeline stepped out of the coffee shop, the morning sun now fully awake and painting the town in a variety of warm hues. There was a soft breeze rustling through the trees on the square, and she could still hear the distant calling of the crows in the forest surrounding them. People were waking up and coming to the square, ready to begin a new day just like she was ready to begin a whole new chapter of her life.

CHAPTER 4

*T*oday, research was the most important thing. Madeline had quickly learned that she could not start writing a book about small-town life until she actually experienced it.

The town square seemed like the best place to do just that. She had already seen the coffee shop, and now she needed to see everything else. She needed to hear the conversations, see the people, and get a sense of what their lives were like. As much as she wanted to go back to her big town life, this was where she would be for the next six months. She needed to think positively about it as much as possible.

The square was picturesque, and it seemed to be the bustling center of life for Jubilee. It did have a lot of character and charm, from the big red brick courthouse in the center to all the storefronts surrounding it. And then there were the mountains in the background that framed the scene in a beautiful way. She pulled out a small notepad that she carried in her purse and started making notes. These were all things that she could describe in her book.

Most of the storefronts had colorful awnings and hand-painted signs. Each building was on the older side, but it gave it a quaint historical feel. She sat down on a park bench out in front of one of the gift shops and just watched for a little while. One thing she noticed was that everybody seemed to know everybody else. As people passed, they would always throw up their hand and wave. They would smile at each other and then stop and chat for a few moments before continuing on with their errands.

After a few minutes, she got up and started walking again. One of the places she had noticed when coming into town was a place called All Tucked Inn. She thought that had to be the most adorable name for an inn she had ever seen. She looked up at the window over the front door and noticed a white dog sitting there, staring at her. It wagged its tail enthusiastically, and that made her smile. She had always loved dogs, even though she hadn't had one for many years. Her constant travel schedule for book signings had made that impossible.

She waved at the dog, completely aware that it couldn't wave back at her. Each time she passed in front of the window, doing her research, the dog would be staring at her, tail wagging.

"I see you've met our town mayor." She turned around to see Brady standing behind her. He was holding a large bag of corn on one shoulder like it was as light as a feather.

"The town mayor?"

"That's Murphy. He belongs to the owners of the inn. He welcomes everybody into town, so we just say he's our mayor."

Madeline smiled slightly. "Cute. Are you following me?"

Brady shook his head and chuckled. "I had to get a bag of corn. I have a lot of animals to feed."

"Right. Well, have fun running your errands."

She walked away, much like he did to her that morning, smiling to herself. She envisioned him standing back there, trying to figure out why she had ended their conversation so abruptly. When she glanced back, not only was he gone, but he was driving down the road. Apparently her little message didn't get through.

She continued to walk, the smell of fresh bread

coming from a local bakery and mixing with the smell of the blooming flowers from the nearby park. She could imagine if there was a welcoming scent, it would be fresh bread and flowers mixed together. She also listened for fragments of conversations as she walked by different groups of people. Gossip was the lifeline of any small town, and she had definitely heard a lot of that.

The noises of a small town were very different from the big city. She could hear dishes being stacked inside the open window of the diner, the gentle hum of a passing tractor, and the playful laughter of children swinging in the park.

She made her way into one of the gift shops, looking at the offerings. Anything from T-shirts to homemade chocolates lined the shelves. Wanting to support local businesses, she bought a bag of chocolate drizzled popcorn and a jar of local honey. She liked to have hot tea in the evenings, and this would be perfect for that.

After checking out some of the other businesses, with the exception of the bookstore, she decided to go back to the house and do some writing. She would go to the bookstore on another day when she had more time because she was certain to get recognized there.

She opened the door to her car, placing the bag in

the passenger seat before sitting down and putting her key in the ignition. She turned the key, but nothing happened. Not even a noise. "Dang it!"

She tried again and again, something she wasn't supposed to do from what she remembered being taught by her father years ago. Finally, she laid her head on the steering wheel and sighed. For once, she felt like writing, and she couldn't make it back to the cabin. Did they even have tow trucks around here? Being in an unfamiliar setting, she had no idea where to go to get her car fixed.

"Are you okay?" She looked up to see Brady standing outside of her window. She opened the door.

"My car won't start. I was trying to go back to the cabin."

"Want a ride?" he asked.

"Don't you have some jumper cables?" she countered.

"I do. But they're back at my house. I just had my truck detailed, so I had to clean everything out."

"Well, that's convenient," she muttered under her breath.

"Or you can call a tow truck, but they service a large area around here. I'm not sure how long you'll be waiting."

"Fine. I would appreciate a ride." She realized she

was being ornery, but she wasn't going to admit that out loud.

"We can just get my jumper cables and come right back. Hopefully, it's just your battery."

"Hopefully." She took her gift bag and her purse, and followed Brady over to his truck. It was giant, and she wondered how she was going to climb up inside of it. Brady opened her door, something she wasn't accustomed to. Her husband had been manly, but she wouldn't have called him chivalrous.

"Do you need some help getting up there?" he asked, a slight smile on his face. Madeline, being as stubborn as a mule, shook her head.

"No, I've got it." She reached up to grab the handle and pull herself up into the truck, but her hand slipped, and she felt herself, almost in slow motion, fall backwards. Instead of landing on the ground, she landed directly in Brady's arms, much like he was holding a baby. For a moment, she found herself wanting to stay there.

"Are you sure you've got it?" he asked, laughing. She wanted to be mad, but right now she was just thankful that she wasn't lying on the asphalt, staring up at the sky.

"Maybe I don't." She was having a very hard time concentrating. He was warm, and he smelled much better than she thought he would being that he ran a farm. Maybe she was expecting that he would smell like a goat, and then she realized she didn't really know what a goat smelled like, anyway.

He slowly released her down to the ground, and she was a little sad. "Let me help you." He held his hand out, and she took it, using it to brace herself as she climbed up into the truck. Once he was sure she was all inside, he closed the door and walked around the truck before climbing behind the steering wheel.

It wasn't until he caught her that she noticed how big and broad his shoulders were. He had a stubble around his jawline and the beginning of crow's feet at the corners of his eyes. His hair was a bit of a mess, and his boots were caked in mud. But for some reason, she was feeling butterflies that she didn't expect.

No. That's not at all why she was in Jubilee. She was there for research, not to lust after some cowboy who caught her when she fell out of a truck. She wasn't that kind of woman. She didn't let her emotions run away with her. She wrote about women like that, but she wasn't one. Every relationship she had ever had was in stark contrast to the romantic ones she wrote about. Maybe there was some psychological reason for that, but she wasn't going to dig too deeply.

"Is that enough air?" he asked, as he pointed toward the vent in front of her.

"Yes. Thanks."

Brady started driving out of the square and onto the main highway that would lead to the road near the house. She didn't know how to make small talk with this perfect stranger, so she just looked out the window, taking in the sights. There was actually a lot to do in Jubilee, from the shopping area to the farmers market to all the nature hikes a person could take. There was a large lake in town, and she had seen at least two marinas where she could rent a boat. Maybe she would do that one day. Take her notepad and her pen, and just float around the lake while she thought about her story.

After driving for a few minutes in awkward silence, Brady finally spoke. "So, where are you from?"

"Atlanta."

"That makes sense," he said, smiling slightly.

"How does that make sense?"

"Well, you didn't know what skeet shooting was."

"I certainly did! But I didn't expect my neighbor to be doing it early in the morning on a weekday."

He held up his hand. "All right, all right. Let's not rehash that. I will make sure to run my skeet shooting schedule past you before I do it."

Madeline rolled her eyes and continued looking out the window. "What's that place over there?"

"That's the park. It has walking trails by the river, a small amphitheater, tennis courts, that sort of thing."

Madeline hadn't expected there was such a nice park nearby. She decided that she would make her lunch one day and sit by the river to eat. "How long have you lived here?"

"Since I was knee high to a grasshopper."

She stared at him. "What?"

"City folk," he muttered under his breath. "I've basically been here my whole life. We moved from a couple of towns over when I was about four years old, but it was much the same as Jubilee."

"So where's your family?"

He cleared his throat like he didn't want to answer the question. "My parents are gone, so now it's really just me." He said it in a low tone like he didn't want to talk about it, and she certainly wasn't going to push him.

"Sorry to hear about your parents."

"You said you were here on a project. What are you working on?"

"My newest novel. Apparently, people only want to buy books set in small towns now. At least that's what my agent and publisher are telling me."

Brady laughed. "That must be a big nightmare for you. So you're here to learn about small town life, but you don't like it, do you?"

"No, I don't. No offense to you, of course."

"Well, that's likely to change."

He turned down the road leading to his house. "Why do you keep saying that? Surely not every-body who visits this town decides to stay and live here. "

"No, probably not. I'm just saying you have to be careful."

"Careful of what?"

He pulled into his driveway and stopped the truck, looking at her. "You gotta be careful because these mountains will change you."

"Oh? Is that so?"

"It is. I've never known a person to live in these hills and not transform."

"And how does one know when the mountains have changed them?"

He paused for a moment. "You'll know when you crave the sound of the creeks and waterfalls. You'll know when only clean mountain air will do. You'll know when you drive into the city or even the suburbs, and there's too many people. Too many cars. Not enough nature. But mostly, you'll know when your heart aches for this place if you're anywhere else in the world because these mountains are home."

Madeline laughed under her breath. "Well, I've never known a place like that, and I don't expect I will."

He smiled, the dimples on both cheeks creeping ever upward. "Nobody ever expects it. It sneaks up on you like a coyote at night. You won't see it coming."

She pulled her body inward. "Are there a lot of coyotes up here?"

"Do you want the truth or do you want to be oblivious?"

"Oblivious, please."

Brady chuckled and then jumped out of the truck, running around the front to open the door for her. "Grab my hand."

"Don't you just need to get your jumper cables? I can wait here."

"I need to take this corn to the barn and check on a couple of things. Here, let me help you." He reached out his hand again, and Madeline took it because it was a nice hand. She really liked his hand the first time she touched it, so why not give it another go?

"What do you mean check on a couple of things?" she asked as she followed along behind him. He already had the bag of corn on his shoulder, and she thought for a moment about asking him to throw her over the other side.

What was wrong with her? She had never been attracted to men like this. Maybe this was what happened after divorce. Maybe some women got hormone surges designed by God to make them want to date again. Surely there was some drug or cream she could get to make her permanently disinterested in the male population for the rest of her life.

Brady didn't answer the question, but instead swung open the barn door and tossed the bag of corn on the floor to the left with a loud thud. The testosterone emanating from his body felt palpable.

"Gilbert, where are you?" he called. Gilbert? Who was Gilbert? Before she could ask him, a small goat came running toward them, making some kind of bizarre noise. It was like he swallowed a kazoo. He stuck out his tongue when he got to Brady and spit at him, still making the loud noise. Madeline backed up a bit and searched her brain on any information related to goat attacks. "There's my boy!"

"I think I'll wait in the truck." Madeline continued backing toward the door.

Brady laughed. "Don't be scared. Gilbert is harmless. I rescued him three months ago from a farm in south Georgia where the owner wasn't taking care of him. Come closer. He doesn't bite."

"But he spits?"

"Yeah, goats are known for their unique personalities. He's all talk, I promise."

She walked a bit closer and watched as Brady loved on the little goat, kneeling in front of him. The goat snuggled his head into the crook of Brady's neck, and suddenly she felt jealous of a goat. That was a new low.

"So you rescue animals?"

"Yep. All kinds. I also do some wildlife rehabilitation."

"Really? Like what?"

"Raccoons, possums, the occasional squirrel."

"You save squirrels?"

He smiled. "I do, when it's needed."

"I'm surprised."

He leaned against the wall of the barn and crossed his arms. "And why is that?"

"I guess I just assumed the men up here hunted animals instead of saving them."

"A lot of men do hunt and provide for their families. I'm not personally one of them, but I can't judge them. All I can do is what I believe in, and that's helping these little guys when they need it." He rubbed Gilbert's head again before feeding him a handful of hay.

A handsome, southern, animal-saving man with muscles. Good Lord, he needed to be a character in her book for sure.

"Is that what you do for a living? Rescue animals?"

"I do have a nonprofit, but I don't make money from it. I mostly do contractor work around here when I'm not volunteering at the fire department. And I board a couple of horses for out-of-town clients. You know, people who live half the year in sunny Florida and the other half here."

A handsome, southern, animal-saving firefighter who's good with his hands and has muscles. She needed some wine.

"Listen, I hate to rush, but I need to get some words written today." As much as she liked looking at him while he snuggled with a goat, she needed to make some forward progress.

"Right. Of course. Let me go grab those jumper cables." Before she could follow him, he was trotting across the yard to his house. Her curiosity wanted to get her inside, to see how he lived. But she knew better. Her job right now was to write a book and get back to the city. She didn't need to make a friend.

Gilbert slowly walked toward her, like he wasn't

sure if she was the crazy one in this situation. When he got closer, she couldn't help herself. She'd never had the chance to pet a goat before, and this seemed like a prime opportunity. She kneeled down in front of him, which in retrospect was mistake number one.

But good old Gilbert kicked things up a notch. He started to make the weird noise that could only be described as a goat-ish yodel, whipped out his tongue, and gave her cheek one long swipe. Caught off guard, Madeline lost her footing and fell onto her back. She blinked her eyes a few times before opening them to see Gilbert standing over her like she was about to be a big goat snack.

"Help!" she yelled instinctively.

"Gilbert, no!" She could hear Brady's footsteps quickly approaching, the hay crunching beneath his boots. Suddenly, Gilbert was gone and Brady was looking down at her, a puzzled look on his face. "Are you okay?"

Madeline dissolved into a puddle of hysterical laughter, which just caused Brady to look more confused. "He licked me!" That was all she could manage to squeak out between laughs. It had been a long time since Madeline Harper had laughed that much. Her stomach cramping, she finally caught her breath and then let out a big sigh.

Brady smiled at her, obviously amused by her predicament. He reached his hand down toward her and she took it, pulling herself up and attempting to wipe the hay off her back.

"Turn around." She turned, and Brady wiped the hay off her back. "There you go."

"That Gilbert is a little Casanova," Madeline said, chuckling.

"He's quite a character," Brady said, laughing. He held up the jumper cables. "Got these. Are you ready to go?"

She paused for a moment before nodding. "Yeah. I should get back." She walked toward the truck.

"Hey, Madeline?"

"Yes?" she said, turning around.

"You look nice when you smile."

CHAPTER 5

*B*rady drove her back into town, jumped her car, and then told her to go to the local auto parts store to get a new battery. She did just that, and she was back on the road to the cabin shortly afterward.

Her time in town and with Brady had given her some inspiration, and she needed to get back to her computer as soon as possible. As she walked into the house, her stomach growled. She'd forgotten to eat lunch in all the craziness of her car breaking down and a goat licking her.

She immediately headed toward the kitchen and went to wash her hands in the deep stainless steel sink. But when she looked down, she saw what could only be described as the world's largest scorpion.

"Oh, my gosh!" she yelled loud enough for the whole county to hear.

Before she could even take any action, her front door swung open, and she saw Geneva running toward her, her long colorful dress flowing behind her. "What's wrong?"

How did this woman get in the house? Was she just camping out in the bushes outside, waiting for any excuse to spend time with Madeline? Back in the city, she would've been down at the courthouse filing a restraining order.

"It's a scorpion!" Madeline said, putting her hands over her face and backing away.

Geneva stopped in her tracks and laughed. "Just a scorpion? Good Lord, child, you scared me to death. I was walking my dog, and I heard you scream."

Likely story. Madeline was still pretty sure she had been hiding in the bushes.

"Just a scorpion? That thing is as big as my hand. I don't know what to do."

"You have to kill it, of course. Those things don't have any redeeming value."

Madeline stared at her. "Kill it? With what? A hammer?"

"No, you can't kill a scorpion by stepping on it or even hitting it with something. They can make themselves flat so they look dead, but they aren't."

"Well, that will be in my nightmares tonight," Madeline mumbled. "So how do you kill a scorpion?"

"You have to stab it with something sharp and pierce its exoskeleton." Geneva said it like she was ordering a pizza. No big deal.

Madeline's nose scrunched up. "You're kidding, right?"

Geneva shook her head. "I'm not kidding. It's the only way. I mean we could get some boric acid..."

Madeline put her hand up. "Please do not finish that sentence."

"Do you want me to do it?"

Yes. Yes she did want her to do it. There was no way Madeline was going to stab a scorpion. She would rather pack her bags and move.

"Yes, please."

"You got a good sharp knife?"

"Help yourself," Madeline said, pointing to the drawer. She quickly ran out of the room, then out of the house onto the porch. A few moments later, Geneva joined her.

"Done. Sent that little sucker to scorpion heaven."

Madeline shivered. "I don't need details. But thanks for doing that. I had no idea scorpions were a thing up here."

"Oh, yes. Just part of the magic of the forest. They

usually like to live in damp dark places, like under logs. But occasionally we do get them in the house. You might want to call the exterminator. They have some pretty good treatments to keep them out. Or at least they usually die within a foot of the door."

Madeline was already rethinking her decision to live here. Six months worrying about scorpions? She would be shaking out her bedding every night before climbing in, for sure.

"I will call today."

"Oh, and be sure to always check your shoes," Geneva said, walking toward the road where her little dog was standing.

"My shoes? Why?"

Geneva laughed. "Scorpions and spiders like to hide in there. Have a good day!"

She watched Geneva walk down the road without a care in the world, and then Madeline went to check her shoes.

YET ANOTHER DAY with no words written. At this rate, she'd be applying for a job as a Walmart greeter any day now. At least she wouldn't have to worry about scorpions and rogue goats. The downside was she'd have to see people and greet them. That wouldn't work at all.

Instead of putting her rear end in the chair to write, Madeline was back in town again, this time at the bookstore. She felt she needed to introduce herself to the bookstore employees since they would surely hear she was in town.

She parked her car in front of the store, which was called Away With Words, and stepped out onto the sidewalk. Each day was getting a little warmer, but there seemed to always be a breeze, which was nice.

The store looked cute with two big picture windows on both sides of the door. Each one had a large display of books. Right now, one side had a collection of timeless romance novels, and the other was a children's book display. Madeline squinted her eyes trying to see if any of her books were included in the romance display, but to her shock none were.

Already a bit peeved at that, she opened the door and walked inside. The place smelled of paper and coffee. It was definitely an older building, and one of the walls inside had exposed brick that had probably been there for a hundred years. There was a checkout counter, a small cafe area with a coffee bar, and what appeared to be a stage in the back. She saw a small sign inviting people to poetry night, so maybe they used the stage for that.

"Welcome to Away With Words!" A young woman appeared from seemingly nowhere, smiling and waving. "Can I help you find something?"

"I'm new to town and thought I'd stop by. What's with the name?"

The woman, whose name tag said Brittany, looked at her for a long moment. "My mama just liked the name…"

"No, I mean the name of this bookstore." Madeline struggled not to roll her eyes.

"Oh…" she said, laughing. "Sorry about that. Our owner is Clementine Carter - we call her Clemmy - and she usually says that books take you away. Away from life's troubles. Away from your worries and fears. So when you come here, we want to carry you *away* with words."

It was actually clever when Madeline thought about it. She wanted to ask how the woman got the name Clementine but feared Brittany might start crying if she asked one more name question.

"Can you point me to your romance section?"

"Sure!" Brittany was way too perky, and Madeline assumed she was probably the head cheerleader over at the high school. She followed her to the back of the store, which was an unusual place to keep the romance books, Madeline thought. After all, they were the most popular genre for people to read.

"I'm surprised you keep romance books all the way back here."

Brittany smiled. "Clemmy says that the ladies want their privacy when they're looking at a romance book." Her face flushed a color of red Madeline wasn't sure she had seen before.

"I see. Do you have any books written by Madeline Harper?" she asked, smiling proudly. This girl obviously wasn't in her demographic, but certainly she would recognize the name.

She thought for a moment. "I don't think so, but let me look." She scanned the shelves and then shook her head. "No, it doesn't appear we have anybody by that name. Is she a new author?"

She shouldn't have let it bother her so much, but she couldn't believe that this bookstore didn't have at least one of her books. How could that be?

"Are you sure? She's a pretty famous author."

Brittany turned around and looked at the shelves again. "I don't see anything. Do you want me to check my computer? Maybe we could order you a copy of something?"

Madeline smiled, trying not to let it show on her face just how much this bothered her. "No, that's okay. But thank you. I think I'll just look around for a bit."

Brittany nodded before walking off toward the front. Madeline looked at every book in the romance section, thinking that surely Brittany had made a mistake. Turns out, she had not. None of her books were there. Her stomach sank. Maybe Laura had been right. She was out of style. Stores were not carrying her books like they used to.

Ten years ago, she could've gone into any bookstore in any town in America, and they would've had her books proudly displayed. Now, she was relegated to discount bookstores, thrift stores, maybe garage sales. But she wasn't in this bookstore. It made her feel queasy. What if she had lost her career forever?

She knew she was probably being overly dramatic, but right now it felt like nobody liked her. She was in this unfamiliar town, this foreign land, and now nobody even recognized her.

She caught a glimpse of herself in the mirror hanging on the wall near the bathroom. Maybe it was just how she looked. She thought she still looked pretty good for a fifty-five-year-old woman in menopause, but she had to admit that there were some extra chins she hadn't expected. She certainly couldn't fit into the clothes she wore ten years ago.

And these days, she had to carry a pair of tweezers in her purse for stray chin hairs. Maybe people failed to recognize her because she didn't look like herself anymore.

As she continued to berate herself mentally, she heard the front door open and Brittany talking loudly and laughing. The next thing she knew, a woman had walked back into the romance area.

"Hey, I'm Clemmy! I own this store, and Brittany said you are new to town…" Before she could finish her sentence, her eyes widened. "Wait. Are you Madeline Harper, the romance novelist?"

Brittany walked up behind her at that exact moment and cocked her head to the side like she didn't understand the conversation. "No, she was looking for some books by Madeline Harper."

Madeline smiled slightly as she continued looking at Clemmy. "Yes, I'm Madeline Harper."

Clemmy clapped her hands and squealed with delight. "I can't believe you're in my bookstore! Right after my divorce fifteen years ago, I started reading your books. I'm a pretty voracious reader, and I got through all of them within a couple of years. You're such a talented writer. What are you doing in Jubilee?"

"Researching, actually. I am thinking of writing a small town romance book."

Clemmy's mouth dropped open. "Really? That would be amazing. I'm embarrassed that we don't have any of your books in stock, but to be honest, sales kind of flatlined a couple of years ago. I'm sure you know that independent bookstores value shelf space, and I just couldn't carry them anymore. I'm so sorry. I'm actually very embarrassed."

Madeline waved her hand. "Don't be sorry. You have to sell what makes you money. I understand. My agent told me that my big city romance books aren't popular anymore. Do you think that's true?"

She scrunched up her nose. "I do. Although I enjoyed them at the time, I'm finding now that most people like small town stories. You know, statistically speaking, most readers are older women. As we get older, we like to reminisce about our childhoods and living in a small town. Maybe that's part of it?"

She had a good point. Not only was Madeline getting older, but so were her readers. While she still loved the city, not everybody was like her.

"Can I ask you for some advice?"

"Of course!" Clemmy said, eager to provide input.

"I need to get plugged in, so to speak, so I can get my research done as quickly as possible. Any suggestions on how to really tap into the pulse of Jubilee?"

"Oh, there are so many ways! I would spend some time at the coffee shop. Everybody in town goes to Perky's. Have you been there?"

"Yes, but just for a short time. I met Ruby Sutton there while she was participating in the quilting circle."

Clemmy smiled. "Oh yes. Miss Ruby is a sweet lady. I would also join our book club. Lots of ladies are members. Oh, and make sure to go to a service at the Baptist church. They are very involved in the community."

Madeline didn't want to tell her that she wasn't particularly religious. She'd grown up in church but hadn't been in many years.

"Those are wonderful ideas."

"Oh, and we have a wonderful rec center with a pool, tennis courts, that sort of thing. It might be a good source of inspiration, too."

"This has been very helpful, Clemmy. Thank you so much. Can you give me more information on the book club?"

"Of course! Follow me to the register, and I'll give you a flyer."

MADELINE DECIDED to go check out the local farmers market before heading back to the house to try to write. She found herself procrastinating, probably because she was out of her element and didn't know what she was going to put on the page.

Surprisingly, the farmers market was a lot larger than she anticipated. It stretched down a long parking lot with covered pavilions end to end. There were all kinds of people there, even for a weekday.

Of course, there was the requisite local produce, but there were also people selling everything from homemade soaps and candles, to large wooden cutting boards. Some of them were quite beautiful and would go for a lot of money back in the city.

She walked around, taking her time to pick out what she wanted to eat for the week. She enjoyed coming here much more than going to the grocery store for her produce. She filled a basket with ripe red tomatoes, red and yellow peppers, and collard greens. She had never been a big fan of collard greens, but she decided maybe she would try a new recipe.

After making her purchases, she got back in her car and started heading toward the cabin. It was a beautiful day, so she decided to take a detour down a road she hadn't gone down before. She was usually pretty good with directions, and she thought this would get her back to the cabin while also allowing her to check out the area.

But as she drove, it became very clear that she was completely lost. Not only that, but she had no cell service, so she couldn't even check her GPS. Thankfully, she still had plenty of daylight left, so she decided not to freak out but try to enjoy the ride.

As she drove down the winding roads, she noticed a place to pull off up ahead on top of a big hill. She pulled her car over and noticed that nobody else was around. She checked her cell phone again, but still no service. Madeline decided to step out of the car and take a look at where she was. That's when she realized that she'd pulled off at a scenic overlook.

She walked across the small parking area to a stone wall, and it took her breath away when she saw the view. Mountain after mountain stretched out before her, all of them tinged in shades of blue. Lush green trees were closest to her, but it was the blue that amazed her. It looked almost like the mountains were carpeted.

She couldn't believe what she was seeing. The sky was completely clear, the sun shining brightly. And right now she felt like the only person on earth. There were no other cars, no other people. She wasn't scared. She felt peaceful. That wasn't something she often got to feel. Her life was always go, go, go.

She closed her eyes and took in a deep breath before slowly exhaling. A couple of years ago, after her doctor had warned her that blood pressure medicine was on the horizon, she'd signed up for some yoga and meditation classes. Those hadn't lasted very long because Madeline didn't know how to relax. Her shoulders were permanently affixed to her ears. In that moment, she felt a peace she didn't know was possible. It must've been the clean mountain air.

When she opened her eyes, she noticed some dark clouds starting to float across the blue sky. She decided that she'd better get back in her car and find her way home before it started raining. It was amazing how it could've gone from such a beautiful day to suddenly seeing rain clouds.

She walked over to the car and pulled on the handle, but the door didn't open. And that's when she saw her keys laying on the passenger seat. She didn't even know how she had managed to leave them there. She was always really good about taking her keys with her, but now here she was on top of a mountain alone, no cell reception, and no way to get into her car before the rain started falling.

A few moments later, the rain appeared. She felt

little droplets falling slowly at first, and then it got heavier and heavier. There was nowhere for her to go unless she wanted to climb down a ravine and get under a tree, and that certainly wasn't happening. She just stood there, like a helpless drowned rat right beside her car. She was so thankful when she saw a beat up old blue pickup truck coming over the hill. She waved her arms frantically, and the older man pulled over, reaching across the seat to roll down his manual window.

"You okay, ma'am?" She wanted to answer in a sarcastic fashion, but she figured since this man was the only chance she had at getting out of there, she wouldn't risk it.

"I got locked out of my car!" she shouted back, over the sound of the rain. She was soaked from head to toe.

"Hop in!" he yelled back. For a moment, she thought about how this man could be a murderer. At this point, she didn't care. She just wanted to get out of the rain. She opened the door and sat down, pulling it shut. It was as heavy as lead. She quickly rolled up the window, forgetting how much power a person needed when rolling up a manual window. Thank goodness for automatic windows and door locks. Well, maybe not the locks. She wasn't super thankful for those right now.

"I'm so glad you came along. The GPS isn't working on my phone, and I don't have any cell service."

He looked at her for a long moment. "Darlin', I don't even have a cell phone. And I don't know what the heck GPS is."

His accent was thick and no doubt southern. He looked like he was probably getting close to ninety years old, if not past it. He was wearing denim overalls, a plaid button-up shirt, and a hat made of straw.

"Do you know anybody who could get my door open for me?"

"Actually, my son-in-law owns a towing company. I suppose we could go to my house and call him."

"If you don't mind, I would really appreciate it."

He nodded his head and grunted a bit before putting the truck in gear.

He pulled over the hill and went down the other side maybe a quarter of a mile before turning left down a long dirt road. It was muddy because of the rain, and Madeline still couldn't believe how quickly it had come on. It went from blue skies to monsoon in the blink of an eye.

"What's your name?"

"Madeline. And yours?"

"Walter. You live here, Madeline?"

"Temporarily. I'm here on a work assignment." She figured it was better to not go into too much detail. A man his age would probably think romance novels were silly.

"What kind of work do you do?"

"I'm a writer." She was hoping he wouldn't ask any more detailed questions, but she certainly wasn't going to lie if he did.

"What kind of stuff do you write?"

"Novels."

"Sounds complicated," he said as he pulled in front of a small farmhouse. The place looked as old as the hills themselves, with a front porch that looked a bit rickety, and a muddy front yard. "I'll go call my son-in-law. You wait here."

Madeline didn't have any problem with that. She certainly didn't want to go inside of his house. "Thank you."

She watched him dodge the mud puddles before walking through his front door, not wiping his feet. She could only imagine what the inside looked like.

A few moments later, he reappeared in the truck. "He should be there in about ten minutes. Thankfully, he was just down the way."

"I really appreciate it. I didn't know what I was going to do. Not much traffic up on that mountain."

"That's why I love it here. Although I've seen it

growing up a bunch since I was a kid. There are so many more people and buildings here these days."

"You've lived here since you were a kid?"

"Right here. My family has owned this land for several generations. That house right there is where I was born and where I grew up."

She had a new appreciation for why the house looked so old and ramshackle. Still, she wondered if there weren't family members who could have updated it over the years.

"Wow! Not many people can say that. Do you have a lot of family around?"

"Just my daughter and son-in-law. My son died over twenty years ago. And my wife died about fifteen years ago. My daughter and son-in-law look in on me as much as they can, but they have their own lives, you know."

"I get it. How many acres do you have?"

"Close to twenty-five acres. Not much to maintain since a lot of it is forest and land."

"It's a beautiful area." Madeline was trying hard to make small talk. She hated small talk.

"Well, I guess we'd better get back over to your car." He cranked the truck, and they drove away from his house. Madeline wondered what it had been like to grow up in the same place for your whole life. She couldn't imagine it.

They pulled back up to her car, and a few moments later, a tow truck arrived. His son-in-law, named Ricky, had her car door open in seconds.

"Thank you so much for all your help, Walter. It was a pleasure meeting you."

"You're very welcome. Be careful getting down the mountain."

Madeline jumped out of his truck and ran straight over to her car. She thanked Ricky quickly and then slid inside, grateful for the comfort of her own vehicle. Meeting Walter gave her an idea for a character; a kindly old man who had lived in the same house for his entire life. These sorts of chance meetings were exactly what she needed to develop realistic characters for her book.

CHAPTER 6

When Madeline got back to the house, the rain had stopped. In fact, the sky was blue again like nothing ever happened. But she still looked like a drowned rat. The first thing she was going to do before she even attempted to write something was take a shower. She couldn't stand feeling so gross.

She went inside, walked upstairs and hopped straight into the shower. She was happily lathering away when suddenly she heard a buzzing noise. She looked around and couldn't figure out what it was, so she continued washing her hair before turning off the water and stepping out.

She wrapped herself in a plush towel and continued looking around the bathroom, not noticing anything in particular but still hearing the buzzing. She brushed her hair, put on deodorant and that's when she saw it. A yellow jacket was buzzing around the bathroom and coming straight towards her.

Screaming, she ran down the stairs towards the front door for some inexplicable reason. Sure she could've locked herself in another room, but panic drove her to get outside as quickly as possible. She ran out onto the porch, breathless, wrapped in her towel. And then something even scarier was there. Brady.

He was standing there staring at her, amusement and surprise on his face.

"What are you doing on my porch?" she shouted.

"I accidentally got some of your mail so I thought I would bring it over. I didn't know I was also going to get a show."

"Not funny. There's a yellow jacket in my house. I was just getting out of the shower, and he was buzzing around my bathroom."

"And so you ran outside in your towel?"

She pursed her lips. "I didn't say it was logical. It just seemed like the right thing to do."

"And if you hadn't already wrapped a towel around yourself? I mean, what was your plan in that scenario?"

She groaned. "This isn't funny. There's a yellow jacket in my house. I might be allergic to those."

"Did you have a reaction in the past?"

"Well, no. But you can get an allergy at any point in your life. You might not be allergic to peanut butter today but be allergic to it tomorrow. Life is like a crazy gamble."

He laughed. "Do you want me to kill it for you?"

"Yes, please. The bedroom and bathroom are just up those stairs."

"Yes, I know. I've been in this house before."

"You have? What, did you date some of the Airbnb renters?"

He crossed his arms. "No, I know the owner. I used to help her with repairs when she needed it."

"Oh." She didn't even know why she made that joke. What did she care who Brady dated?

"I'll be right back."

He went into the house and up the stairs. A few moments later, he came down with a dead yellow jacket in a piece of toilet paper and flipped it over the side of the deck, putting the toilet paper in his pocket.

"Thank you. This house is a bug haven. Geneva had to kill a scorpion in my kitchen sink."

"Did you call the exterminators?"

"I did. They come next week. But what are they

going to do about a yellow jacket? Where did that thing even come from?"

"Well, if you have a yellow jacket in your house, there's a good chance you have a nest in the ground around here."

"In the ground? They're coming up out of the ground?"

"Usually. We can walk around the property and see where it is if you want. Or I can leave you to figure it out yourself."

"Let me get dressed, and we'll walk around the yard. Or you can walk around the yard, and I will stand up here on the safety of the deck and watch you."

He smiled. "I figured that might be the case. You're not exactly an outdoorsy kind of gal."

She looked up at him. "And how do you know that?"

"You almost had a heart attack about a yellow jacket, so it's pretty evident that you don't spend a lot of time out in nature."

"Or maybe I've just never had the chance to. Maybe I'll start hiking since I'm up here for six months."

"Oh, you want to hike? I do that all the time. I can take you out on one of the trails."

"We'll see."

She walked into the house and up the stairs so she could change clothes. What had she just done? Agreed to possibly go on a hike with Brady? He was right. She didn't like the outdoors. She was not a nature kind of person. But now she had somehow managed to agree to become one.

By the time she came back downstairs, she saw Brady down in the yard standing near a tree. "Found your problem," he called up to her.

"Well, get away from it. You don't want to get stung!"

He waved his hand. "I work on a farm, Madeline. I'm not scared of bugs."

"Those things are little flying devils. They are beyond bugs."

Brady joined her back on the porch. "We need to buy some gasoline."

"Excuse me?"

"That's how we get rid of the nest."

"Have you been drinking this morning?"

He laughed. "You're so untrusting. Listen, you can call an exterminator and wait a week for them to come, or you can do it the mountain way."

"With gasoline?"

"Yes. We wait until the sun goes down, pour gasoline in the hole, and then that's it. The gas puts off a substance that kills them."

"Do we light it on fire?"

"No. We just have to do it at the right time."

"And if we pick the wrong time?"

He paused for a moment. "Let's just do it at the right time."

Madeline cleared her throat. "How'd you like to come to dinner tonight?"

He looked at her, surprised. "Sure. Can I bring anything? Wine? A dessert?"

"Gasoline."

MADELINE COULDN'T BELIEVE she'd invited Brady to dinner, but there was no way she was pouring gasoline in that hole by herself. Cooking him dinner seemed to be the least she could do if he was putting himself in danger on her behalf.

She finished the sauce for the spaghetti and pulled the garlic bread out of the oven. Madeline had never been a great cook, but she could at least make a decent spaghetti dinner. Hopefully Brady liked it.

Just as she was setting the pan of bread on top of the stove, she heard a knock at the door. At least he was better than Geneva who always wiggled the handle before knocking. That woman had no boundaries.

She opened the door and Brady grinned as he held up a can of gasoline. "I brought the wine!"

"You're so funny," she said, rolling her eyes. "Put that on the end of the porch. It stinks."

He set the can of gasoline on the other end of the porch and then followed her inside. "Something smells good."

She waved her hand. "Well, it's not you. You smell like the gas station."

"Oh, sorry. A little must've dripped on my boot." He took off his boots and tossed them outside.

"Hope you like spaghetti."

"Who doesn't?"

She went into the kitchen to finish making the tea while Brady sat on one of the tall bar stools at the breakfast bar. "You like tea?"

"Sweet tea?"

"Is there another kind?"

He leaned forward and whispered. "I hear up north, those folks drink tea without sugar in it. What a bunch of nutcases, huh?"

Madeline couldn't help but laugh. Brady had a great sense of humor. I mean, the guy owned a goat named Gilbert, and that said a lot for his ability to laugh.

"So, the sun goes down in about twenty minutes. Are you ready for the big yellow jacket takedown?"

"Of course. I've done it a million times."

"I don't understand all your mountain ways."

He chuckled. "Mountain people have had to take care of themselves for a long, long time. My ancestors lived in these hills for generations, and they were strong people. They didn't have grocery stores or fast-food places. They didn't have TV or fancy phones. But they were happy, and they were all about family. That's what I admire most about them."

"That's very nice. I'll have to add it to my book."

"How's that coming along, by the way?"

She leaned against the counter. "I'm sure it would be better if I'd write some words. So far, nothing is coming to me."

"Maybe that's because you haven't gotten involved enough."

"You're probably right. I'm thinking of joining the book club."

"That's a good idea. I think you also need to see the sights. Really get in touch with nature."

"As you have seen, I'm not so much into nature."

"You probably haven't been exposed to it enough."

"Listen, a scorpion and a yellow jacket was enough exposure for me."

"Speaking of that, I guess I'd better go get ready

for my invasion." He stood up and walked to the door, stopping on the porch to put his boots back on. "If I don't come back alive, tell Gilbert I loved him… most of the time."

She slapped his arm. "That's not funny. I don't want to inherit Gilbert!"

She could hear Brady laughing as he walked to the end of the porch and picked up the gas can. Without missing a beat, he walked straight over to the tree, bent down, poured the gasoline in the hole and then ran like heck back to the porch. To Madeline's surprise, nothing happened. No yellow jackets came out of the hole.

"Done," he said, striding across the porch like a cowboy. He leaned against the log wall and smiled. "Anything else, little lady?"

"Ha ha. Where are the yellow jackets?"

He stared at her for a moment. "Yellow jacket heaven? Or maybe the other direction? It really depends on how they acted in this life."

"So they're dead? Just that easy?"

"If I had done that an hour ago, I'd be stung all over. It's really just a timing thing."

"How weird," she said, opening the door to the house. "I thought it would be more dramatic, honestly."

Brady followed her inside. "So you wanted me to get stung?"

She laughed. "Maybe just once."

BRADY LEANED back in his chair and groaned. "I ate way too much. You make a mean spaghetti, Madeline Harper. You should put that in your author bio."

"I'm sure it would be impressive," she said, laughing. She took a long sip of her wine. Brady had gone to his truck just before dinner and brought in a bottle. He had good taste in wine, which was unexpected.

"So, tell me about yourself."

"Like what?"

"Well, I know you're an author, and you like the big city, but what else? Ever married? Prison time?"

She laughed. "Divorced recently. No prison yet, but there's still time, I suppose. What about you?"

"Widowed."

Her heart caught in her chest. "I'm so sorry."

"Thanks. It was a long time ago. She had a congenital heart defect that caught up with her. We were high school sweethearts."

"What was her name?"

"Nicole. She was a spitfire. Red hair, mean temper. But she loved me, and I loved her."

"No kids?"

"No. With her heart issues, we didn't think it was wise to bring a child into the world just to become motherless."

"That was a hard decision, I'm sure."

"It was. She would've made a great mother. What about you? Kids?"

"No. Just wasn't in the cards for me."

"You have family around?"

"Well, that's complicated. I have a father who remarried when I was in high school to a woman who didn't want me around. I haven't seen him in a long time."

"Sorry to hear that. And your mama?"

"We have a tumultuous relationship. She never liked my choice of careers."

"Being an author? Seems a mama would be proud of that."

"She thought being a romance author was embarrassing to her at the church."

Brady let out a laugh and then covered his mouth. "I'm sorry. That was just the most ridiculous thing I've heard in a while."

"Same here."

"Do you write... you know... smut?"

Madeline's mouth dropped open. She tossed a piece of her garlic bread across the table. "No! Are you serious?"

"I had to ask!"

"It's just that mother thinks writing about romance is silly, and she didn't want her friends to know. Of course, then I became a household name, and her friends found out, anyway."

"So why not have a relationship?"

Madeline sighed. "Who wants to have a relationship with someone who judges you so harshly? It's exhausting. She's been this way my whole life. Always making me feel bad about myself. One day, I'd just had enough."

"I get it. Any siblings?"

"Nope. You?"

"I had a sister, but she's gone."

"I'm so sorry."

"Boy, this conversation is kind of a bummer," Brady said, laughing.

"I'm not so good at small talk."

"I'd better get home, anyway. I need to feed the animals before I head to bed."

"You go to bed this early?" she asked, looking at her watch.

"When you work on a farm, you have to get up early."

"True."

Brady stood up and walked to the door. "Thanks again for dinner. I don't get a lot of home-cooked meals."

"I'm not a very good cook, but I'm glad you enjoyed it."

"Don't knock yourself, Madeline. You're better than you think you are."

"Thanks."

"Goodnight," he said softly before walking out onto the porch. She watched him get into his truck and drive away, and for a moment she felt immediately lonely. Maybe she hadn't realized just how much she needed someone around.

MADELINE FINISHED CLEANING up from dinner and went upstairs, tired from her adventurous day and ready to go to sleep. She slipped into her PJs and then into her bed, turning off the lights completely. That wasn't something she normally did. Usually, she turned on mindless TV in the background, set a timer on her TV, and fell asleep at some point. Her TV back home would turn itself off.

Tonight, she was feeling ready to sleep, though. Thoughts of Brady wafted through her mind, and she pushed them away. She wasn't in Jubilee for a relationship, even a close friendship. She would be leaving in a few months, and forming close bonds with anyone wasn't on the agenda. She was here to save her career, end of story.

It was a beautiful night, so she opened the window to allow the cool mountain air to flow into her bedroom. As Madeline lay in her bed, she began to drift off into dreamland. The big, wooden house was creaking slightly, almost like it was falling asleep itself.

Living in the city had given her the ability to deal with noises, but suddenly she heard unfamiliar sounds. The chorus of the night was an ensemble of insects and other critters that she could not name, each creating a weird but perfect harmony. But there was one that stuck out above the rest, and it was keeping her awake.

It had a high, rhythmic call that almost sounded like music. It kept a beat like a drum. Sound resonated around her bedroom, filling the room and then her brain. She had never heard anything like it before with its clear, sharp rhythm that echoed in her ears and only paused a moment between each call. It was pitch black dark, but this bird sang with enthusiasm, shattering the silence of the dark Georgia night. The calls were meant as a serenade for the moon and the stars, but she was also an unwilling listener.

Madeline put a pillow over her head, willing to chance smothering herself just to get some sleep. But still the sound permeated the pillow and threatened to drive her insane.

Annoyed and exhausted, she decided to investigate the source of the noise. She wrapped her robe around her and ventured onto the deck outside her second-story bedroom. It was so much louder outside. It was like the bird was inches away, trying to get her attention.

She walked to the corner of the porch, trying to follow the ethereal notes. The sound seemed to come from everywhere and nowhere at the same time. It bounced from one tree to another, swirling around in the cool Georgia night air. She looked at each tree, squinting her eyes as if she could see much. It was pitch black in the forest at night, the only illumination coming from the moon and stars.

That's when she saw the flutter of wings as something moved from one tree to another, seeming just as interested in her as she was in it. It disappeared into another tree on the other side of the yard and resumed its song. The rhythm never changed. Madeline felt like she could dance to it if she was a dancer. That was not a skill she possessed, unless it was slow dancing. That she could do.

She retrieved her phone and typed what she was hearing into the search bar. A whippoorwill. It was a nocturnal bird known for its repetitive and distinctive song. She tried to ignore the part that said some considered its presence to be a harbinger of death.

Madeline leaned against the half wall of the porch that abutted the roofline and stared out over the mountains. She could see little lights dotting some of them, which were probably the lights on in houses and cabins.

She looked up at the dazzling display of stars blanketing the sky like diamonds. She didn't see that in the city. There was too much light to be able to see the stars, and she had to admit she was shocked at how many she could see tonight.

She stood there listening to the sounds of the forest. The whippoorwill was still making its noises, but it didn't bother her so much now. There was a comfort in the sound. She walked over, sat on the glider that was on the deck and started pushing herself back-and-forth in rhythm to the sound of the whippoorwill.

Over time, its call softened, and somewhere along the way Madeline fell asleep. It was the deepest sleep she'd had in a long time. There was so much to worry about with her business and her failed relationship that she hadn't realized just how stressed she'd been for so long. That was until the whippoorwill sang her to sleep on her porch.

When she opened her eyes, she was shocked to find the sun peeking over the mountains, bringing with it streaks of pink and yellow.

The sound of the whippoorwill was replaced by the cawing of the crows that had descended on her backyard. She stretched her arms high above her head and yawned. That had to be one of the best nights of sleep she'd had in a while, even though she wasn't in a bed and didn't have a pillow.

"Good morning!" She looked down from her porch toward the road and saw Geneva standing there with a large insulated thermos in her hand. "I brought my special coffee!"

"How did you even know I was out here?"

"I saw you up there during my morning walk. I've been up for a couple of hours."

"Let me get some clothes on." Madeline really didn't want company this morning. She had hoped to get up, make some breakfast and start writing. But Geneva had other plans.

She threw on a pair of yoga pants and a T-shirt before heading downstairs and opening the door.

Hopefully Geneva didn't get too close since she hadn't even brushed her teeth yet.

"I was surprised to see you sleeping out on the porch," Geneva said as she walked into the house. She went straight over to the kitchen table and sat down, opening the piping hot thermos of coffee. Madeline grabbed a couple of mugs from the kitchen counter and joined her at the table.

"It was unintentional. I heard this noise outside last night, and it wouldn't stop."

Geneva chuckled. "You must mean the whip-poorwill. I call him Gus."

"How do you know it's a male?"

She poured a cup of coffee for Madeline and slid it over to her. "Typically, it's the males you hear at night in the eastern United States. He's trying to find a mate. It's the call of romance."

Madeline laughed. "Last night I wished I knew how to use a BB gun. Or that I even had a BB gun."

"I think it would be bad luck to shoot a whip-poorwill. I certainly wouldn't chance it."

"You seem to believe a lot of things about nature and the mountains."

"Well, I did grow up here. Not too many miles from here is the homestead my family lived on for generations. When everyone died out, I bought this place because I just couldn't take care of the other one. They built the new library on our old homestead. Made me a little sad. Progress can be a tough thing."

"I met a man named Walter yesterday who grew up here. Lives in the same house where he was born, and he's in his nineties. He helped me out when I locked my keys in my car on top of the mountain."

"There's a few of us old-timers still here. But yes, I love these mountains. I love nature. That's why I do herbal medicine and wilderness hikes."

Madeline didn't know how old Geneva was, but she guessed she was in her early seventies. It really surprised her she was hiking those woods. Seemed like it could be treacherous for someone who was in good shape, much less someone of her age range.

"So you make herbal remedies?"

She nodded. "I take what God provides in nature, and I turn it into healing. You know, some preachers around here do the laying on of hands. I do the same kind of thing, but God gives me the ability to heal with what He put here for us."

Madeline took a sip of the coffee and almost choked. "Goodness! What is this?"

"It's my own special blend of coffee beans, with added chicory and dandelion root."

"It's so strong," Madeline said, walking to the kitchen to get some cream.

"Maybe for the uninitiated," Geneva said, chuckling. "I have to get going, but I wanted to invite you out for a hike. Maybe this weekend?"

"I don't know…"

"Oh, come on! If an old bird like me can do it, so can you. Think what you'll learn for your novel, too."

"Fine. Saturday morning?"

"I'll come by at six-thirty." Geneva took her thermos and walked toward the door.

"Why so early?"

"These mountains get hotter as the day goes on. Might as well meet Mother Nature as soon as she wakes up. See you Saturday!"

Madeline watched Geneva walk down the road before she poured her cup of "coffee" down the kitchen sink.

CHAPTER 7

*A*s expected, Geneva showed up bright and early Saturday morning. Madeline was both excited and nervous about their upcoming hike. The last couple of days, she had been head down trying to get some writing done. There were moments where the words flowed freely, but she wasn't accustomed to a small town life yet, so it took her extra time to think through the scenes she was writing.

When she wrote about the city, it was easy to describe the skyscrapers and the nighttime lights. Those were things she had looked at for most of her adult life. But now she was going to go tromping around in the forest, and that just seemed like a crazy thing to do. Still, it was something she felt was necessary so she could put the details that were important into her new book. After all, readers were very smart at picking out those things that weren't accurate. She wanted to sound like she came from a small mountain town herself, so this was just another piece of the puzzle.

"Are you ready for this, city girl?" Geneva asked, when they arrived at the beginning of the hiking trail. The trail they were going to was pretty close to the house, and Madeline was thankful for that. There were lots of hiking trails around Jubilee thanks to its proximity to the national forest.

Geneva wore olive colored hiking pants, a pair of boots, and a black T-shirt. Her wiry gray hair was sticking out at all directions, but she had a scarf tied around it to keep it out of her face.

Madeline stood there in her borrowed hiking boots, which were at least a half a size too big, and felt the fear weighing heavier on her back than the giant backpack Geneva had strapped to her.

The sun was already casting streams of light through the trees. "We want to get in and get out by lunchtime."

"Why?" Madeline asked, fearful that there was something dangerous that happened at lunchtime.

"Because I have a vegetable stew in my slow cooker, and I'll be hungry by then."

Madeline sighed and rolled her eyes. "You scared me."

Geneva studied her carefully. "You can't be scared. The forest won't accept that."

"What in the world does that mean?"

"It means that animals can sense fear, and you'll put us both in danger if you go wandering in there putting out those vibes."

"Vibes? Were you a flower child?"

"Were?" Geneva said, laughing. "Anyway, there's nothing to fear."

"Snakes, bears, those wild hogs, yellow jackets, Bigfoot…"

Geneva put her hand on Madeline's shoulder. "Honey, things are going to happen no matter what you do. You can't spend your life fearing stuff."

"I most certainly can. What if a snake slithers across the path in front of me?"

"Snakes don't want any part of you. Make noise. They aren't interested in being noticed. Leave them be." Geneva made it sound so easy. "You ready now?"

"As ready as I'll ever be."

She followed Geneva on the leaf littered path. As they made their way deeper into the forest, Geneva pointed out plants. Madeline tried to listen, but mostly she was looking for those yellow jacket nests in the ground.

"That right there is jewelweed." She pointed toward a plant that had yellow flowers. "It can help soothe a rash from poison ivy."

"I hope to never have poison ivy," Madeline said, suddenly aware that any of the greenery currently surrounding her could be poison ivy, and she wouldn't have a clue.

"That over there is a sycamore tree. The inner bark can be used as a mild analgesic."

"Uh huh," Madeline mumbled as she watched the ground for snakes. How anyone found this to be a relaxing hobby was beyond her. The entire time, she felt like she was looking out for snipers.

Still, as Geneva talked, Madeline started picking up on some of the wisdom that she had accumulated over the years. She thought about how Geneva's ancestors probably had lived, needing this wisdom out of necessity. She also watched as the older woman maneuvered the forest like it was nothing. She didn't look down and focus on the ground. She was looking sideways and up. She marveled at every tree and bush and flower she came across. While Madeline saw a giant wall of vegetation and possible danger, Geneva saw a pantry, a history book, a pharmacy, and a sacred space.

"This right here is ginseng. It's very important in our area and has been used for centuries as a medicine." The plant didn't really stand out to Madeline, except that it had bright red berries. If she had been out here alone, she certainly wouldn't have thought anything of it other than worrying that it might be poisonous. Geneva carefully took a small portion and explained that she was leaving plenty of the plant so it could continue reproducing. "We only take what we need. When it comes to nature, balance is the most important thing."

They continued walking along for over an hour, Geneva pointing out plants, insects and even the occasional deer. Madeline could see that she was getting tired, and she herself felt the need for a break.

"I see a stream up ahead. Maybe we could sit down for a bit?"

Geneva nodded. "Yes. I think that would be a good idea."

They sat down on a large, flat rock right next to the bank of the stream. Geneva reached into her backpack and pulled out an insulated mug, full of hot tea. She gave it to Madeline to take a sip.

To Madeline's delight, the tea was normal and didn't have a weird taste to it. She was worried Geneva was going to put something in there that tasted like dirt or leaves.

"It's beautiful here."

"The world doesn't know what the deep parts of the Blue Ridge Mountains hold. I believe it holds the secrets to life, but nobody stops long enough to notice."

"And Bigfoot?" Madeline said, laughing.

"You're making a joke, but many folks up here believe. Shoot, many people around the world believe they've seen him."

Madeline cut her eyes from side to side, now on alert for a big hairy man-beast.

"How long have you been hiking?"

"Oh, since I was a little girl. My Pop - that's my dad - used to take me out in the woods and teach me things. He taught me how to identify plants, how to know which snakes were venomous, that kind of thing. He learned from his grandmother."

"Generations of knowledge. Was your family religious?"

"Oh my, yes. I am, too, even though it might not seem like it. I look at these hills as gifts from God. I don't worship the mountains, but I revere them. I cherish them. But I still pray every morning and every night. Two things will save you in this life - the prayers you send up and the roots you put down."

"That's beautiful, Geneva." She wished she'd brought her notepad to write that last part down, but instead Madeline left those words in the forest.

It was such a profound statement. What roots had she put down? Here she was, living in another place for six months, divorced, no kids. She had no roots.

"What you need to understand is that this forest is an ecosystem all on its own. It operates like one of your big cities, and you'd never know it unless you look closer. Every plant, every insect, every bird has a role to play. We also have a role to play by staying out of their way and not harming them."

"Of course."

"Speaking of birds, you do know it's not wise to put out bird feeders, right?"

"Why is that?"

"Bears will travel for miles for food, and bird feeders are probably their favorite next to trash cans."

"I have been keeping my trash cans in the garage."

"Well, avoid bird feeders."

Madeline didn't have the heart to tell her she had two out in the backyard. She felt certain no bear was going to travel to get to her little bird feeders when there were so many other tasty trash cans along the way. "Got it."

"You ready to head back?"

Relieved, Madeline nodded her head. She'd enjoyed the hike a lot, but she was ready to get out of the ill-fitting hiking boots and into a nice, hot shower. "Yes. Let's go."

As they walked back, Geneva regaled her with stories of growing up in the mountains. Tales of her grandmother killing a wild boar with an ax, learning to cook at her mother's feet, learning to fix a car motor with her uncle. Even though Madeline still preferred bright lights and tall buildings, she was starting to see the allure of small town life. It offered a lot more than she'd thought.

Geneva's beat-up old pickup truck rattled as they drove down the gravel road. The lingering excitement from having completed her first hike still fresh in her mind, Madeline was suddenly jarred out of her positive mindset when she saw white smoke billowing from the direction of Brady's farm.

"That's Brady's cabin!" Her heart was hammering against her breastbone. The sight of smoke out in the middle of the forest was terrifying. And where was Brady? Was he inside?

Without another thought, she swung open the door of the still moving truck and jumped out. Geneva was calling behind her as she screeched to a stop, but Madeline was already way ahead. She ran through the thick brush toward the open space of Brady's farm. The hiking boots she'd borrowed threatened to slip from her feet as she sprinted, but she was thankful running had been a pastime of hers in her younger years.

Geneva walked quickly behind her, but Madeline was already standing just feet from the house by the time Geneva came out of the brushy area. Madeline pulled her phone out and immediately called the fire department, having to describe where the farm was since she still didn't know the names of all the roads.

"Call Brady!" Madeline yelled back to Geneva. She knew she'd have his number, and she prayed to God he wasn't inside. The fire was growing so fast; it wasn't safe to knock on the doors or look in the windows.

By this point, the smoke had been replaced by orange flames shooting out of the attic area of the house. Madeline looked around until she found the garden hose and then turned on the spigot, trying in vain to make the water reach the second floor. It was terribly inadequate for the job. The attic was far outside of the reach of the water.

"He's not answering his cell phone. I'll try another number where he may be," Geneva called over the sound of the crackling fire. They both backed up from the house.

Suddenly, Madeline remembered Gilbert. Where was he? She ran to the barn, which wasn't far from the house, and immediately found him. Luckily, the horses were already in the furthest fenced area, but she pulled on Gilbert until she got him in the same area. She ran back for a baby pig Brady had recently rescued and put it in with the horses and goat. She hoped they all got along. Were pigs and goats natural enemies?

After getting the animals squared away, Madeline's gaze drifted back over to the house. The smoke was getting thicker and thicker, changing from white to an angry black color. Flames were attacking the old wooden structure. She couldn't remember what year Brady said the home was built, but she did know it belonged to his grandparents. When he was young, his parents had moved them closer to his grandparents, and he'd eventually inherited the whole property.

Madeline was aware of Geneva standing right next to her, but both of them were silently watching the scene playing out in front of them, awaiting the scream of sirens that seemed to be taking an eternity to arrive. She knew it had only been a few minutes, and they were coming as fast as they could, but it didn't seem to be enough. She wanted to do something, anything. This was the most helpless she'd ever felt in her whole life.

As the fear and adrenaline started to dissipate, the women were left with the grim reality of what they were looking at in front of them. Thankful that the animals were at least safe, although confused, Madeline felt like she had at least done something for Brady in the midst of all the chaos. She had acted as quickly as she could, making sure to save the things that were most important to him. It might've been a small victory, but every little victory counted right now.

Finally, they could hear the distant sound of sirens, and then the bright red fire trucks arrived on scene. Lights were flashing urgently as the fire-fighters with heavy gear jumped out before the vehi-cles. They unraveled their hoses with efficiency and began to work on the fire, mainly to contain it. The house was obviously a total loss.

Geneva put her arm around Madeline, probably in an effort to comfort her since Madeline could feel her face contorting. Neither of them spoke, but she knew they were both worried about Brady. Where would he live? How would he react? He was a big part of the Jubilee community, so Madeline had no doubt that the locals would rally around him quickly.

Out of nowhere, a cloud of dust arose from the opposite direction, Brady's familiar pick up truck screeching to a halt. Madeline was relieved to see him, if for no other reason than to make sure that he wasn't actually inside the house. He jumped out of his truck and walked toward them, his eyes as wide as saucers. He was breathless, but unharmed, thankfully. He immediately looked at Geneva and Madeline, the three of them staring at each other in the middle of the sea of chaos going on around them.

The firefighters continued to battle, but it was containment that was the goal. There was no way any part of this structure was going to be saved. Madeline walked closer to Brady, explaining about moving the animals and calling the fire department. She told him what she'd initially seen with the smoke and that they'd tried to use the hose. She knew she was blathering on and on, but it was because she didn't know what to say. Her instinct was to wrap him in a hug, but that seemed highly inappropriate given she didn't know him that well. Geneva had no such notions. She immediately pulled him into a big, motherly hug, and Madeline felt a bit jealous.

"Oh, honey, I'm so sorry. We did everything we could."

"I know you did. I don't know what could've happened. I suppose it could've been the wiring…" He stared at the burning house in front of him, obviously wracking his brain for some kind of reason this was occurring. "I know these guys are doing everything they can." Being a volunteer firefighter himself, Brady just happened to be off that day. Madeline knew he felt helpless.

"I'm so sorry, Brady," Madeline said. For a word-smith, she was experiencing a major lack of words right now.

"Thanks for getting the animals to safety."

"I really didn't do much. I was just afraid the fire would spread to the barn."

"I appreciate you moving them. It's what I would've done, too."

His face was so pained that it was hard for Madeline to look at him. She knew while she was watching a house burn, he was seeing memories of his entire life going up in flames.

"Is there anything I can do for you?"

He smiled and shook his head slowly. "It's just going to take me some time to process all of this. That home meant a lot to me. It was my grandparents' home, and then my parents' home. I can't tell you how many memories I had there, and to watch them all burn right in front of me is a little more than I expected to happen to me today."

"Hey, Brady. Can I talk to you a minute? I have some questions," a firefighter asked as he walked over to them.

Brady nodded his head. "I am."

"We just have some things we need to talk to you about. Can you walk with me for a minute?"

As Madeline watched Brady leave to talk to the firefighters, her stomach churned. She barely knew the guy, but her heart ached for him. Why did bad things happen to good people?

CHAPTER 8

*M*adeline and Geneva stood on Geneva's back deck overlooking the woods. She really didn't have a good view of the mountains themselves, but she said that she liked being tucked away under the trees, having shade any time she walked outside.

Her house was smaller than Madeline had imagined. It was more of a cottage in the woods with one bedroom, living room, bathroom and kitchen. She also had an enclosed porch where she kept all of her essential oils, tonics and potions. Geneva's decorating style could only be described as eclectic, with colorful modern accessories mixed in with very old family heirlooms.

"Do you think Brady will show up?" Madeline

asked, craning her head towards the front of the house to see if she could spot his truck.

"Oh, he'll come. He knows better than to tell me a fib." Geneva continued staring straight ahead, looking at a pair of crows flying through the forest, chasing each other.

"How long have you known him?"

She smiled."Since he was a little kid. I was friends with his mother. We went to church together."

"I think I see his truck."

The two women walked back through Geneva's house and met Brady on the front porch. He was carrying what appeared to be a cherry pie. How on earth had he managed to get a cherry pie when his house just burned down?

"Good evening, ladies," he said, smiling. How was he smiling? Madeline would've been curled up in the fetal position under her bed if her house had burned down. Well, probably somebody else's bed since hers would likely be gone.

"You made a cherry pie? How?" Madeline said instead of saying hello.

He chuckled. "You know they sell these at the grocery store, right?"

"Yes, but I wouldn't have thought you had time to go to the grocery store. Your house just burned down, Brady."

"I'm aware. But that's still no reason to have poor manners when you come to somebody's house for dinner." Acting like it was completely normal that he went out and bought a cherry pie while his house was still smoldering, Brady walked past them and into the house. Geneva shrugged her shoulders and followed him into the house.

"Do the firefighters have any idea what caused it?" Geneva asked as she took the pie from Brady's hand and set it on the counter.

"Not yet. They have to send the investigators. It might be a week or two before we really know. Insurance is already working on it."

"Where will you stay in the meantime?" Madeline asked.

"I have a barn. I can sleep there."

"There's a bed in the barn?"

"Well, no. But I can make it work. What's that great smell?" It was obvious to Madeline that he didn't want to discuss the fire anymore, so she decided not to bring it up. They would all act like nothing had happened, apparently.

"I cooked my famous garlic chicken served over creamy noodles."

Brady grinned and pulled Geneva into a tight hug. "My favorite. I'm so glad you remembered."

"When Brady was a little boy, he used to love

eating this meal. He also loved my fried chicken and meatloaf, if I remember correctly."

"Do I need to burn something else down to get both of those?" Brady asked, laughing. How could he be joking at a time like this? Madeline would've been devastated if something like this had happened to her. It was his childhood home and belonged to his grandparents. She just didn't understand how he was already kidding around about it.

"You know, I have space here if you'd like to stay. I mean I only have the one bedroom, but my sofa is always available."

He smiled down at her. Brady was a tall man, and he towered above both of them. "I appreciate it, but I'll be fine in the barn. I need to be as close to the animals as I can."

"Well, just know the offer is always open."

They walked over and sat down at the kitchen table to chat while the chicken finished cooking. Geneva's home was just like she was - eccentric, charming and chock full of curiosities. It was nestled into the woods like it was meant to be there, like the trees were growing around it. It was a small wooden structure, weathered but strong. Outside, vines climbed up one side of it, and colorful wind chimes hung on all corners of the porch, filling the air with melodies.

Inside of the home, it seemed like every surface was covered with one of Geneva's collections. Dried flowers, colorful crystals, old maps, stacks of books. She seemed to collect a little bit of everything. It was like stepping into some kind of strange museum. Each item in her home felt like it had a story to tell, and Geneva was surely the one to tell it. There was a corner hutch that stood across the room, looming over everything with its dark wood and the glass doors. It was filled with all kinds of jars and bottles, each filled with their own particular potion, some of them vibrant colors. It gave a special light to the room.

The smell of fresh baking bread wafted through the room, drawing each of their noses upward. "Is that bread?" Madeline asked.

"Oh yes. My mother and grandmother taught me how to make the best yeast rolls in the whole south. I bet you won't have had anything like them. Slather some butter on, and it'll make you wanna slap your mama."

"Slap my mama?"

Brady laughed. "That's a pretty common old southern phrase up here. Yeah, you don't say that in the city?"

"I haven't heard it," Madeline said, slightly smiling. "It's not a popular phrase in my normal crowd."

The kitchen had herbs hanging from the ceiling, bringing with them smells of pine and earth that seemed to permeate the house. The dishes on the counter were a series of mismatched plates and bowls, some with vibrant colors and others just a plain white.

It was like Geneva's home was perfectly perfect for her, and no one else could ever pull it off. What would've normally looked junky and mismatched looked like it was made for Geneva. Madeline tried to imagine Geneva living in Madeline's more modern city home, and she just couldn't see it. Geneva would never fit there.

Once dinner was ready, Geneva made everyone a plate and brought it to the table. She just wouldn't hear of anybody coming into the kitchen and making their own. She grabbed a large pitcher of sweet tea from the refrigerator and poured everyone a glass. She was the consummate hostess, although Madeline would've never expected it.

As they ate, the conversation flowed naturally with Geneva telling stories of Brady's youth, like the time that he and his buddies got into old Mr. Hudson's moonshine stash. Or the time that Brady fixed his grandfather's old tractor, but it got away from him and rolled down the hill into the neighbor's duck pond. Her favorite story was the one where a teenage Brady convinced his friend that the neighbor's old outhouse was haunted, so his friend went inside on a dare one night and sat on a porcupine who was sleeping there.

Of course, Brady talked about Geneva and all her potions. He even brought up her late husband who Madeline had never heard about. His name was Gordon, and he was the love of Geneva's life for over thirty years until he passed away several years ago. Her eyes watered as she talked about him, and Madeline wondered what it was like to have a love like that. That was not what she had experienced with her husband. It was much more surface level, not soul level.

Madeline talked about writing books and what that was like. They asked her all kinds of questions about where she came up with her story ideas or how many words she could write in a day. She told them about her trips all over the world doing book signings, and even that one time when a celebrity mailed a copy for her to sign. She told them that she was still having trouble with her small town book, and Geneva suggested she get more plugged into things going on in town. Meet more people. Make more connections. She knew it was true, but she hated to do either. She was going to leave here in just a few months, so she didn't want to form strong bonds. Although tonight, she felt like she had formed two already.

Brady also talked about the farm, the history it held for his family, and the animals he loved. He talked about Gilbert and all of his crazy antics. If Madeline didn't know better, she would've thought Gilbert was his child. As they talked, Madeline made mental notes for characters in her own book. She marveled at how much Brady and Geneva both loved the Blue Ridge Mountains, and how it seemed they were inextricably tied to those hills for the rest of their lives.

While Madeline loved the city, she didn't feel a pull to it like these people did to their mountains. She could live in a big city anywhere in the world, and it would've been fine with her. But these mountains were special to these people. There was a connection. A relationship between them and the nature that surrounded them. For a moment, she envied that. She realized that most of her life had been about writing those kinds of connections for other people to read, but never having them for herself.

Brady was deeply rooted in this land that he called home. And Geneva seemed to be a part of it. She was like one of those trees planted in the forest behind her house. Her roots were so deep, she couldn't be removed from it.

"Should we have some of that cherry pie?" Brady asked, leaning back in his chair.

"I couldn't fit another bite in my stomach!" Geneva said, her hand on her midsection.

"Same for me. I never eat this much." Madeline wasn't a big eater. She normally ate salads, and the occasional steak or piece of chicken. This was a lot of food, and carbs, for her. In fact, she felt like she needed a nice long nap.

When dinner was over, they cleared the plates and walked out onto the front porch. The sun was setting, streams of orange and pink visible through the trees. Brady, who had been so talkative when he first arrived, seemed to have gotten quieter. She could see that sadness was weighing on him, and she watched him as the weary slump in his posture appeared.

"I have something for you," Geneva said, pulling a vial out of the pocket of her dress. She handed it to Brady. "I made you this tincture. It's valerian root, passionflower, and just a touch of honey. It'll help you sleep. Put a spoonful in some warm water before you go to bed."

He took it from her hand. "Thanks, Geneva."

As they all said their goodbyes, Madeline walked

Brady to his truck. Geneva, sensing that they needed a moment alone, walked back in the house and shut the door. Madeline only had to walk next door, but Brady had to drive down the gravel road to his farm.

"Are you sure you're going to be okay sleeping in the barn?"

He looked down at her. "I've slept in worse places."

"I'm really sorry about your place, Brady. I wish there was something I could do."

"You and Geneva already did it. Good night, Madeline."

OVER THE NEXT FEW DAYS, Madeline worked on her manuscript as diligently as she could. Some of the things she had already experienced with Geneva and Brady, especially, were giving her ideas for her book. She made notes, wrote, and then rewrote. But at least her fingers were moving across the keys. Sometimes, mostly at night, she sat out on the porch outside her bedroom and brainstormed onto a pad of paper. The most important thing was her creativity was starting to come back, and for that she was very grateful.

This evening, though, she was leaving home to go

to the book club meeting that Clemmy had invited her to. The bookstore wasn't quite big enough to have a club meeting, so Clemmy explained that it was in one of the extra rooms on the lower floor of the historic courthouse. Situated directly in the middle of the square, the dark red brick building rose straight up from the green, grassy lawn.

She parked her car on the square and stood under the stately shadow of the historic building. She felt a wave of nerves running through her body. It was kind of silly when she thought about it, especially given that she had done speeches in front of crowds of readers many times over the years. And now she was nervous about going into a small book club meeting in a mountain town?

She supposed one of the things she was nervous about was the fact that she hadn't had a chance to read the book. But Clemmy assured her it was fine to come and get to know some of the other women in town.

She entered the room, which was a surprisingly open space that had bookcases along two walls and some comfortable couches. She'd expected a stuffy old room with some folding chairs, so this was actually an upgrade. The old brick walls gave the room a very rustic charm, like many of the buildings in town. At least a dozen women had already gathered, having animated conversations with each other. They were laughing and chatting, hugging and waving. Clemmy, with her cool haircut and trendy glasses, was presiding over the gathering of fellow book lovers.

"Madeline, glad you could make it! Come, I want you to meet some of the members."

Madeline walked over and forced a smile. As many times as she had been around the world doing book signings, and making small talk with strangers, it still didn't get any easier. She was an introvert at heart, but sometimes she had to suck it up and interact with people. In reality, she had spent so many years with the characters in her head that she was much more comfortable chatting with them.

"Hey, Clemmy. Thanks for inviting me."

"Madeline Harper, this is June. She used to run the book club, but she decided to retire a couple of years ago and hand it off to me." She pointed at the short, rotund woman who was standing beside her. She had fire engine, obviously dyed, red hair. She also loved her make up, given the fact that the pink lipstick she was wearing almost blinded Madeline.

"Oh, honey, I'm so glad to meet you! I can't tell you how many of your books I've read over the years."

"That's wonderful to hear. It's very nice to meet

you," Madeline said, smiling. At least it was good to hear from someone that they had read her books. Since she had come to town, she felt almost invisible. Back in the city, she got recognized a lot more often, although not as much these days as ten or fifteen years ago.

"And this is Dolores. She's our oldest member of the book club."

"Stop telling people that!" She was obviously a spitfire, even though she probably didn't stand five feet tall.

"Do you mind if I ask how old you are?"

"I'm ninety-six years young. And if Clemmy doesn't stop telling everybody that I'm an old coot, I'm going to smack her on the behind!" She playfully swatted at Clemmy's read end.

"I'm sorry, Dolores. I'm just so proud of how well you get around."

Dolores rolled her eyes. "What's the alternative? Lay in my bed? I refuse to do that. If the good Lord wants to take me out, he's going to have to do it while I'm walking."

Madeline chuckled at that. "I think you have a wonderful attitude."

"Well, I'm going to go get my chair before somebody steals it," Dolores said, wandering off.

"She's a hoot. All the ladies here are wonderful. I think you're really going to enjoy it," Clemmy said.

"I'm a little nervous because I didn't read the book. Just don't call on me," Madeline said, winking at her.

Madeline went and found a seat next to Dolores, and Clemmy walked to the front of the room to get the meeting started. There was a pause in the conversation as Clemmy introduced Madeline. She received a mixture of warm smiles and curious glances from the diverse set of women who seemed to range in age from their mid twenties all the way up to their nineties. Madeline had found over the years that reading could bring together any group of people who otherwise wouldn't normally interact.

The discussion was about a book called "The Only Way", which appeared to be a story about a woman who finds out that her late husband has been the head of a crime ring, and she is forced to restart her life while she's also in danger.

Madeline listened as the women discussed the book. Some points were actually very interesting, and she knew that she would have to read the book once she had some free time.

"I think the character arc of Sally was amazing. I mean, in the beginning of the book, we see a naïve housewife, but when we ended the book, Sally was a strong, independent woman," a young woman said. Her name tag said Jenna, and Madeline remembered her being introduced as a local schoolteacher.

"I agree, but I didn't like that part in the middle where she kept doubting herself," Dolores piped in. "That part really dragged for me."

Madeline listened to everything they said, fascinated by their interpretations and how deep their insights were. As an author, she had never been involved in a book club, so it was interesting to see what readers thought about different tropes, tones and ways of doing things in a piece of fiction.

After the discussion about the book, they broke for some snacks and coffee, allowing Madeline to have conversations with some of the other women. There was Delilah, who had formerly been an artist in New York City, but now lived in this rural landscape. Her husband had been transferred a couple of years ago to an adjoining town about half an hour away. Delilah was still adjusting to living in the mountains. She was in her forties and had the most boisterous laugh Madeline had ever heard. She reminded her of a younger Geneva with her vibrant clothing and matching personality.

Madeline also got drawn into a discussion between a mother and daughter who were both members of the book club. The mother was a native to the mountains, and the daughter had gone away to college and come home for a visit. They talked about their shared love of books, and it made Madeline think about her own relationship with her mother. She tried not to think too hard about that because there wasn't much she felt she could do at this point.

"How are you liking Jubilee?" She turned to see Dolores standing beside her, holding a cup of punch.

"It's beautiful here."

Dolores rolled her eyes. "Just because I'm an old lady doesn't mean you can't tell me the truth."

Madeline was shocked. "I'm sorry?"

"When you're as old as I am, people tiptoe around you. They don't say what they're really thinking. Of course Jubilee is beautiful. That's not what I asked you. I want to know how you like it here."

Madeline nodded. "It's been a challenge. To be honest, I love the city. I love the honking horns and the bright lights. I didn't think I would like it here at all. I didn't like it at first, but it is actually growing on me."

"I can understand. I was born here, but I spent over thirty years living in Boston. My husband had a very successful legal firm there. At first, I had a really hard time adjusting to city life, but once I did, I loved it. It was hard to leave when we came back here."

"Wow. I never would've imagined you lived so far away."

"Let me give you a piece of old lady advice. You can love living in a certain place, but that doesn't mean you have to stay there forever. We are meant to explore. We are meant to meet new people. And it's not about the place. When you're at peace with yourself, anywhere can be home. When you're with the right people, that is your home. It's not those lights or those buildings or those honking horns. It's hard to leave the familiar behind, but without doing that, you may never find what God has for you."

"That is wonderful advice, Dolores. I'm glad I got to meet you tonight."

She smiled and took the last sip of her punch before tossing it in the trashcan beside them. "I'm glad, too. Who knows? The Lord can take me home tonight, and I'll be off on my next adventure. But for right now, I'm glad I got to meet you also, Madeline Harper."

As she watched the older woman slowly walk to the door, she felt a stirring in her heart. Jubilee was getting to her, and that was something she never thought would happen.

CHAPTER 9

The morning sunlight filtered through the wooden blinds, leaving long thin shadows on the floor of the cabin. The scent of the fresh mountain air along with the sound of crows, a familiar refrain, woke Madeline. She did her normal morning routine of brushing her teeth, showering, and making a pot of coffee before finally arriving at her desk in the loft. This had become one of her favorite places to write because she could look out the giant windows of the living room over the mountains. It gave her inspiration for her book.

She opened her computer to reveal the blinking cursor. The book was moving along better than it did at the beginning, but she still had a long way to go. There wasn't a day that she felt one-hundred percent confident that she was going to be able to write a small town book, but she was trying. That was all she could ask of herself. Certainly, it would still be easier to write a big city book. It was what she had known for over twenty years. But she was starting to ease into small town mountain life much more than she thought would've been possible.

Going to the book club had given her such a better feeling of what small town life was really like. The relationships, the way that community members really leaned on each other. Back in the city, everybody was moving so quickly, and it wasn't about community as much as just moving through your life and getting things done. People didn't have time to sit and chat and wave as much as they did in a small town.

For some reason, she had slept restlessly last night, so she was already starting off on the wrong foot today. Her mind felt like a muddled mess, but she had to do her work. That was one thing she had learned as a writer many years ago. It didn't matter how she felt. She had to get up and speak for her characters because otherwise they couldn't speak for themselves. It was her job, and she took it seriously.

However, after a good half hour of futile attempts to get any words on the page, she pushed her computer away and closed it. Another thing she had learned years ago was not to force it. Her readers would always be able to tell when she was just writing fluff. And she refused to write fluff.

Madeline believed in making every word count when she wrote a book. She wanted her readers to really feel something, to feel connected to the characters and the storyline. So if she sat down and just phoned it in, they would be able to tell.

She sat and stared out the window for a few minutes, taking in some deep breaths and trying to do a mini meditation. She still wasn't good at it.

Remembering that she hadn't checked the mail the day before, she decided the best thing to do was to take a break, hop in the golf cart and ride down the road to check her mail. At least it would give her some time outside where she could hopefully clear her head and wake up a bit.

She climbed into the golf cart, backing it up to the loud piercing sound of the reverse beeping. She had to figure out a way to turn that off. It was one of the most annoying sounds she had ever heard.

She puttered down the dirt road, which was slightly steep in places. She listened to the sound of the tires crunching the dirt and rocks below it, and the rustling of the leaves from the wind this morning. It was actually a bit chilly, but what was one to expect when you were over two-thousand two-hundred feet up?

She finally made it down to the bank of mail-boxes that sat at the end of the road. She hopped out, grabbed her stack of mail and turned the golf cart around to head back up the hill. It only made it about one-hundred feet before it suddenly screeched to a halt.

"What in the world?" She turned the golf cart off and on again. Nothing. That's when she noticed she had no power. Searching in her mind, she realized that she probably hadn't plugged it in the last time she used it. How in the world was she going to get up the steep hill back to the house? There was no way. She obviously couldn't push the thing. Looking around, she saw nobody. No cars. No neighbors. There was only one option. She was going to have to walk through the woods and see if Brady was at the farm. He was the closest option. And of course, she didn't bring her cell phone.

She got out and rolled the golf cart over to the side of the dirt road, just in case anybody else needed to drive their vehicle through there. She put the key in her pocket, put the mail in the storage compartment in the back and started her walk through the woods. Luckily, there was a little trail, so that she didn't have to climb through vines and briars. She knew that there was probably poison ivy or poison oak, but she tried not to think about it since she had no idea how to identify it. She watched the ground carefully, so she didn't step on any snakes. Knowing that there were rattlesnakes in these woods was enough to terrify her.

This day was just conspiring to test her patience. First she had writer's block, and now her golf cart died. She hoped this wasn't a sign about what the rest of the day was going to be like. And, she was taking a chance that Brady was not even going to be home. She didn't see his truck, but it was possible that it was parked on the other side of the barn.

The first thing she saw was Gilbert, who was standing at the edge of his fenced area, looking at her with his tongue hanging out. Her grandmother would've said he was so ugly, he was cute. She wasn't sure that was even true. Gilbert was missing at least two teeth, and his eyes were two different colors. Madeline had to laugh when she looked at him.

"Isn't he handsome?" She turned to see Brady standing behind her, a dirty rag in his hand.

"Where did you come from?"

"Originally?"

"Very funny. Why are your hands so dirty?"

"Changing the oil in my truck. It's over there." He pointed to a covered carport on the other side of the lot. She had never noticed it before.

RACHEL HANNA

"I need your help. My golf cart died before I could get up the hill."

He laughed. "You didn't plug it in, did you?"

She shook her head. "I forgot again. Can you help?"

"I have a portable charger we can use. Let me go get it."

Madeline followed him over to the barn. Along the way she noticed a red cat, so she leaned down to pet it.

"How are you liking living in the barn?"

"Well, I mean it's not the Ritz Carlton. I guess it will do."

As Brady went to look for the charger, Madeline glanced upstairs. All she saw was a pillow and a blanket. She slowly walked up the stairs while Brady wasn't looking, and she couldn't believe what she saw. There was a small battery operated lantern, a pillow, a makeshift mattress and a blanket. When Brady had told her he was sleeping in the barn, she assumed there was some finished space upstairs, but he was really sleeping in the barn like the animals. She walked back downstairs.

"Brady, are you actually sleeping up there?"

"Yes. I told you I was sleeping in the barn."

"You can't sleep up there! There's not even any

air conditioning. And you don't have a real mattress. That can't be comfortable."

"It's fine. The animals do it every day."

"You're not an animal. You can't do that. You don't even have a real bed."

"Madeline, like I told you, I've slept in worse places before. It'll just be a few months."

"Absolutely not!" She held up her hand. "You'll stay in the basement at my cabin. I'm sure the owner won't mind. She knows you."

"I appreciate the offer. But I'm not doing that." He turned around and went back to looking for the charger.

"Yes, you are. You'll be able to check on the animals just as easily being right up the street. You'll have your own space downstairs with the bedroom, living room, bathroom and a kitchenette. It'll be like your own bachelor pad."

He laughed. "You're not going to leave this alone, are you?"

"I'm very stubborn that way."

"Okay, if you don't think it will be an imposition. Just try not to run around wearing your towel. My heart can only take so much."

MADELINE WATCHED as Brady maneuvered the golf cart down the hill onto his farm like it was nothing. He waved over his shoulder before he disappeared around the other side of the barn, and a small sigh escaped her lips. What on earth was she thinking? Why in the world would she invite the most handsome man she'd ever seen to live in her basement?

She finished walking up the hill to the cabin, thinking about all of these things. Brady had offered to drive her there, but it was just a short walk and she needed to clear her mind. In a couple of hours, he would be living in the house with her, and she didn't know how that was going to go.

She had extended the invitation to Brady out of concern for the fact that he was sleeping in the barn with the animals. But now she couldn't shake the worry that this might lead to something more and she was the one in danger of making a big mistake.

It had been a very long time since Madeline had felt this way about any man. Maybe she had never really felt this way at all. Even with her husband, there had never been a deep, abiding love there. Madeline had settled, and she knew it from the moment she said I do. She was also a loyal person, and she wasn't going to betray her marriage, so she stayed. She stayed until Jacob made the decision - by cheating.

The marriage had been comfortable, but always devoid of passion and love like she wrote about in her novels. They had mundane conversations, very little in common, and they were comfortable in the silence that descended upon their home like a cloud. They very rarely even had a heated argument, and now looking back, she realized that was because there were very few emotions between them. They had lived a practical life. A part of her didn't blame him for ending the marriage, although she did blame him for how he did it. She wished she'd had the courage to end it years before.

When she finally made it to the cabin, she walked inside and found herself standing in front of one of the big picture windows overlooking the mountains. She couldn't help but think about Geneva and how she talked so highly about her late husband and the wonderful marriage they'd had. Madeline was sad that she had never experienced that, never known a love so deep that she would still mourn the passing of the person even years later.

Why was she so able to put emotional scenes together with fictional characters but she wasn't able to put together a real relationship in her own life? And maybe that was why she was so fearful about letting Brady stay at the house. She knew there were feelings there she had not had with Jacob, even in the earliest parts of their relationship.

Or maybe she was just making all of this up in her own head. Maybe she was just so starved for love and affection that she was planting the idea that Brady was even interested in her. And no matter what, she couldn't be interested in him. She was going back to the city in just a few months.

Her relationship with Jacob had been more of a partnership than a marriage. He'd been her assistant, the person who organized her tours, and an extra set of eyes on every book. They did not have that love-filled bond that a married couple should have. Those years were bittersweet when she thought about them.

She walked over to the kitchen and poured herself a glass of iced tea. Her mind was filled with worry about Brady moving in. She could see herself falling for him with his kind nature and his chivalrous charm. He was different than any man she'd ever known, and way too similar to some of the heroes she'd written about in her books. Sure, they hadn't been farmers or cowboys. They'd been big city businessmen, but they had still been heroic and chivalrous. He was thoughtful, kind and full of surprises, and it was surprises that scared Madeline the most. She liked things she could prepare for, and falling in love was not one of those things.

She imagined that a relationship with Brady would be deep and abiding. More than she could handle.

She was here to write, and that was the end of it. There was nothing more that could be had in Jubilee. She couldn't make strong friendships, and she certainly couldn't fall in love. She was there to learn about the simplicity of small-town life so she could get her career back on track, and she couldn't allow anything to derail that.

So why did she invite him to live there? Brady was rough and tough, and he was certainly able to live in the barn if he had to. But she felt this need, this responsibility, to invite him to stay there. Was it for him, or was it for her?

"Wait. So you invited the hot farmer guy to come live in your basement?" Laura asked from the other end of the phone. Even though she was Madeline's agent, they had become close friends over the years.

"First of all, his name is Brady. And from what he told me, he's been friends with your aunt for years."

"That's definitely true. I remember her

mentioning Brady before. But the question is, why did you invite him to stay there?"

"Because he was sleeping in a barn. I told you that."

"Madeline, you're only there for a few months. You're supposed to be focusing on your career. Do you really think this is a good idea?"

Madeline sighed and leaned back in the over-stuffed recliner, looking at the ceiling. "No, of course it's not a good idea. He's like a hero right out of one of my romance novels. But I just couldn't leave him sleeping in the barn like some sort of animal."

"I'm sure he has other friends or family in the area. You weren't the only option."

"Yes, but I live right next door to his farm. He has to take care of those animals several times a day. It just made the most sense."

Laura wasn't buying it. "Whatever you say. My aunt doesn't mind, of course. She loves Brady. From what she says, everyone does."

"I'm glad she doesn't mind."

"Just be careful, Madeline. You've had your heart broken a couple of times lately, and I don't want to see it happen again."

Her heart was more broken by the publisher not taking her book than by her husband's infidelity, but she certainly didn't want to tell Laura that. It made her sound like a horrible person.

"I'll be careful. Listen, I need to go. Brady just pulled up with my golf cart."

She pressed end and walked outside, just in time for Brady to turn off the golf cart. He'd kept it down at his house long enough to get it charged up, and he was plugging it in when she walked outside.

"She just needs a good long charge and then she'll be fine."

"Thank you for doing that. I don't know what I was thinking. I'll always remember to plug it in at night from now on."

"Listen, I wanted to talk to you."

"What's up?"

"I want to give you another chance to bow out of me staying here. You don't have to do that, and I will totally understand if you'd like to change your mind. You're trying to write a book, and I know you must need your space."

She shook her head. "I'm not changing my mind. You're the only thing I have resembling a friend in this town. What kind of person would I be if I let you sleep in a barn?"

"You have Geneva," he said, laughing.

"True. I think I was looking at her as more of a mother figure," Madeline said, biting her lip.

"If you're sure you don't mind, I'll just go back and get my things. I'll feed the animals and then head up here in a couple of hours if that works?"

"That works great. I was thinking about just making sandwiches for dinner. Something simple. Is that okay?"

He laughed. "You know, you won't have to prepare dinner for us every night. I don't expect that. I can make myself something down in the kitchenette. There's a microwave, right?"

"Brady, it's just sandwiches. I'm not making you a Thanksgiving turkey or a rack of lamb. I know I don't have to make food every night for us, but since it's your first night, I figured I'd make it easier."

"Thanks. Sandwiches are fine. I'll have to cook you dinner one night." He turned and started walking towards the road.

"Are you a good cook?"

"It's one of my hidden talents," he said, holding up his hand and waving as he disappeared behind the trees.

adeline finished making the chicken salad and put it in the fridge just as she heard Brady's truck in the driveway. This was it. He wasn't just coming for dinner. He was coming to live there.

She opened the front door and smiled. "Hey, roomie!"

Brady laughed. "I promise I won't play my music loud, and I'll put the toilet seat down."

"Well, that would make you every woman's dream man." She watched as he pulled a duffel bag from his truck. "Is that all you brought?"

He paused a moment. "It's all I have left."

What was she thinking? "I'm sorry. I don't know why I said…"

"It's fine, Madeline," he said, walking up onto the porch. "I don't get easily offended."

"Good, because I tend to put my foot in my mouth a lot."

He followed her inside and set his bag on the back of the loveseat. "Thanks again for offering to let me stay here."

"You aren't going to thank me every day, are you?" she asked, laughing.

"Maybe."

"Dinner is almost ready. I'm just letting the chicken salad get cold in the fridge. Wine?"

"Sure."

"How's Gilbert today?"

"Confused, I think."

"Because of the fire?"

Brady chuckled. "No, because he's Gilbert."

Madeline laughed. Gilbert was the epitome of interesting. If he was a person, they would probably seek mental help for him.

"He's adorably ugly," she said, handing Brady a glass of wine.

"I'm not sure that's a thing."

"Do you want to go sit on the deck?"

"Sure. I'm always up for staring at the mountains."

They walked out onto the deck and sat in the two

rocking chairs overlooking the beautiful view. For a moment, Madeline thought about how this was how people felt when they got older and were sitting in rocking chairs with the love of their life.

She wondered if she'd ever have that.

"So, how are you feeling?"

"You mean about the house?"

"Yes."

"I've had some time to think about it, and I have to admit I've shed a few tears thinking about my grandpa sitting in the back room watching TV. Or my grandma in the kitchen making her famous chicken and dumplings. But I also know that every good thing eventually comes to an end."

"Do you really believe that?"

"I do. It might not come to an end until we pass away and go to heaven. Or it might come to an end somewhere in the middle of our lives. You just don't know. I'm thankful I wasn't hurt and that my animals weren't hurt, either."

"That's a good way to think about it."

"So what do you think? About all good things must come to an end at some point?"

"That seems to be the way it's going for me. My marriage, my career."

"Your career isn't over, Madeline. You're just having a little bump in the road."

She chuckled. "It doesn't feel like a bump in the road. It feels like everything is falling apart, and I don't know if I can get it back together. I know it sounds shallow or even egotistical, but people used to recognize me. I got stopped all the time because I was interviewed on TV many times. I used to be invited to book signings all over the world. And now it's like I'm invisible. I think that happens to women of a certain age."

He shook his head. "That's insane."

"Excuse me?"

"You're not past your prime, Madeline. How old are you?"

"You shouldn't ask a woman that question, but I'll answer it, anyway. I'm fifty-five. And you?"

"I'll turn fifty in a few months."

"It's very different for men. You become more distinguished as you age. We women have a lot to keep up. We're supposed to look like we're twenty-five when we're fifty-five. It's unfair and exhausting."

"Well, given that you're one of the most beautiful women I've ever seen, I don't think you have to worry about any of that."

Her heart rate sped up. It had been a very long time since any man had told her she was beautiful. It wasn't exactly something her ex-husband said all the time.

"Thank you."

"I don't know why your self-confidence is so low right now, but from what I see, you have a lot to offer. You have readers that have loved you for years, so I'm sure they will flock back when you release your new book."

"I guess so. I think the divorce really did a number on my head."

They had talked a little bit about her divorce at dinner, but she didn't go into great detail.

"How long were you married?"

"Right at twenty-five years."

"Wow. That's a very long time. Mind if I ask what happened?"

She knew it was bound to come up, eventually. Part of her didn't want to tell anyone because she felt like it made her look bad that her husband chose some other woman, but she felt like she needed to be honest.

"He was having an affair with my best friend. So I lost my husband and my best friend, both of whom worked in my business, at the same time."

"What an idiot. He obviously didn't know what he had."

She didn't know what to say to that. This was feeling like a very intimate conversation between the two of them, and Madeline was determined not to start anything up with Brady. She was just lonely, simple as that. She needed to focus on having a friendship with him and nothing else.

"I played my part in it. I was never really in love with Jacob, but I couldn't admit it to myself. And then he was so involved in my business that I just let it go on and on. I'm glad it ended, although I'm not happy about the way it went down."

"You're a very nice person, Madeline. I hate to think that you were in such an unhappy marriage for so many years. That had to be torture."

She smiled slightly. "It wasn't as bad as you think. I've spent most of my life escaping into characters that I created in my head. Maybe that makes me mentally ill."

He laughed loudly. "I don't think so."

"My husband's biggest complaint was that I was too focused on my work. I spent too much time with my characters, and not enough time with him. I can't say that he was wrong."

"Well, it seems to me that he didn't hold your attention like your characters did. It's fine to love what you do for work. And if you really wanted to spend time with him, I'm sure that you would have. Sounds to me like he wasn't holding up his end of the bargain by being interesting enough to pull you away from your books."

Madeline smiled. "I guess that's one way to look at it. I hate that you've had to go through so many things in your life, and now the fire."

"I've had a good life so far, so I can't complain. When I lost Nicole, I thought my life was over. But then as the years went on, I was able to find other things to make me happy. The animals, the farm. Being a part of this community. It saved me."

Madeline's stomach churned. She hated that these bad things happened to Brady, of all people. He seemed to be one of the good guys. And now she wondered if he felt sad that he never had children. Not that it was too late for him. It was certainly too late for her.

"I can't imagine. And you have spent the rest of this time alone?"

"I've dated, of course, but let's just say the options are limited up here in the mountains. Not that many people live here, and most of them are old or married."

"I don't have that problem in the city. I guess when I go back, I'll get on one of those fancy dating apps and try to find a guy who doesn't have two heads or sixteen kids somewhere."

Brady smiled. "What am I going to do when you go back?"

"You survived all these years without me here. I think you'll do fine."

He didn't say anything else, but looked out over the mountains for a few minutes, watching as the sun set. Beautiful shades of pink and orange were painted across the sky, like God had a paintbrush in his hand and was creating it for them in real time.

"You know, there has never been a time where I got tired of looking at that view."

"I can understand that. I didn't think I would enjoy it here, but getting to look out over the mountains anytime I want is very soothing. I'm not great at relaxation, but I can sit here and look out there and feel a little sense of peace."

"Well, I'd better go downstairs and unpack. I need some sleep. Staying in the barn didn't exactly lend itself well to get eight hours of sleep each night."

"I understand. I need to go do some writing before bed."

They got up and walked inside, Madeline locking the door behind them. Brady chuckled because he knew nobody locked their doors up there, but he didn't say anything.

"Well, good night, Madeline."

"Good night, Brady." She watched as he opened the door to the basement and then closed it behind him, the sound of his boots hitting each one of the hardwood steps on the way down. Whether she liked it or not, butterflies flittered around inside her stomach. This was going to be a long few months.

As THE DAYS PASSED, Madeline and Brady got more accustomed to living in the same house. He mostly kept to himself, except for early in the morning when she would meet him in the kitchen for a cup of coffee. Some days, usually weekends, he would be gone most of the day. Madeline assumed he was working at his farm, but she didn't ask. It was none of her business.

It didn't take them long to get into a routine, and it made Madeline feel a lot better. She was so worried there were going to be all of these awkward moments, but they were really starting to develop a friendship.

Of course, she couldn't help but notice how attractive he was. Early in the morning, late at night. It didn't matter. Brady Nolan was the best looking man she'd ever seen. He had laugh lines around his mouth, small crow's feet forming around his eyes, and stubble that seemed to grow every evening. He had strong, masculine hands that weren't always perfectly clean. His boots always had a little bit of mud on them. His jeans looked like they needed to be replaced. But all of it together made him very attractive.

She was in menopause, so she thought her hormones would be pretty much nonexistent by now, but apparently not. Every time she looked at him, she got a chill up her spine. She couldn't remember that ever happening with anyone else, and she thought about calling her doctor.

On this particular morning, Madeline decided to go into town to eat at the local country cooking restaurant. It was called The Rustic Spoon, which she thought was a fabulous name. She walked in and saw that the place was pretty busy given that it was lunchtime. The aroma of home cooking wafted across the room and made her incredibly hungry.

"Hi, honey. How many?" The hostess, who had jet black hair done up like a bouffant on top of her head and the bluest eye shadow Madeline had ever seen, smiled.

"Just one."

"Madeline?" She turned her head to the left and noticed Geneva sitting alone at one of the booths. "Why don't you join me?"

"That would be great."

She walked over and slid into the booth across from Geneva.

"What are you doing in town today? I figured you'd be back at the cabin writing."

"I was going a little stir crazy. I just needed to get out of there for a while. Otherwise I get writer's block, and then I can't get out of it."

"Well, I just ordered, so let me wave the waitress back over here." Geneva held up her hand, and the woman came running back over to the table.

"What can I get you?" She was young, probably high school age, with blonde hair and a long ponytail.

"I think I'll just take the salad with grilled chicken…"

"No, you won't!" Geneva said, shaking her head. "If you really want the small town experience, you need to eat the food we serve here. She'll have the meatloaf with mashed potatoes and collard greens," Geneva said, taking the menu out of Madeline's hand and giving it back to the waitress. "Oh, and sweet tea."

"Aren't you bossy?" Madeline said, laughing.

"Honey, nobody up here is ordering a salad with grilled chicken. They just have that on there for the yuppies that might come through during tourist season. If you really want to learn about living up here, you have to experience the culture."

"I'd like to leave in the next few months without clogged arteries."

Geneva rolled her eyes. "Live a little, Madeline. You're missing out on life."

Madeline stared at her. "What is that supposed to mean?"

"I just came from my doctor's appointment. Every time I go to the doctor, they tell me how old I am and what new thing is breaking. Skin is getting thin. My bones are getting weak. I need to have my cataracts checked. Do you know how demoralizing that is?"

"I'm sorry. I know that has to be hard."

"If we're all blessed enough to live a long time, we'll all go through it. But you know what I never do? I never look back and wish I'd had less fun."

Madeline smiled. "I guess that's true."

"You're only fifty-five years old, and that is young to me. At your age, I was kicking up my heels having a good time. You should be doing the same. You should be in love, relaxing, having fun. You've paid your dues. You've worked hard. I just don't understand why you hold yourself back so much."

"Well, you're just full of opinions today, Geneva." Madeline wasn't getting angry, but it was making her feel uncomfortable because Geneva was right. She never did anything fun. She worked, she ate, she slept. None of that was particularly interesting. Even back in the city, she was never super involved in a lot of stuff because she wanted to keep writing her books. It was much easier to live vicariously through her characters than to try to build a life that she actually enjoyed.

"I'm sorry. And I know I haven't known you that long, but I think sometimes other people see us for who we really are. I think that's why Brady likes you. He sees the real you that you still can't see."

"What do you mean that Brady likes me?"

Geneva smiled. "See? That's the first time I've seen you get a little excited about something. He's not bad to look at, is he?"

Madeline reached across the table and slapped Geneva on the hand, but then she realized that Geneva apparently has thin skin and it made her feel bad.

"I did not get excited. I just asked a simple question."

"I think you like him."

"He's a good guy. Everybody likes Brady."

"You know it's more than that. You're just scared."

"Geneva, I've only known him for a few weeks.

And I'm only here for a few months, max. If I finish my book early, I might even leave sooner. It doesn't matter whether I think Brady is cute or I like him, because nothing is going to happen."

"How are you set financially?"

"Excuse me? Did the doctor give you some new medication or something?"

"What I'm really asking is do you have to write more books? Or could you live off your royalties?"

Madeline swallowed. "I suppose I could live pretty well off my royalties. I saved a lot of money over the years."

"So what if the real reason you ended up in Jubilee wasn't to reinvigorate your career? What if it was because God had your true soulmate here, and He orchestrated all of it so that you would have to cross paths?"

"I really think you're grasping at straws."

Thankfully, the conversation was broken up for a few moments when the waitress brought their drinks. She told them their food would be ready in a few minutes, and Madeline couldn't wait. First of all, she was starving, but secondly she wanted some food in Geneva's mouth so she would stop talking.

"Listen, I'm not trying to butt into your life."

"I think you are," Madeline said, laughing.

"I adored my husband. We had so many

wonderful years together. And I guess I'm just looking at you, and I'm looking at Brady, and I'm seeing two people who should obviously be together. I want you to have what I had."

Madeline reached over and put her hand on Geneva's. "And I appreciate that, but you don't know what my life was like back in the city. I have no plans to move to Jubilee, so there's no reason to start anything with Brady. I wouldn't want to break his heart or my own. It just wouldn't work. He's not moving to the city, and I'm not moving here."

"Oh, I wouldn't be so sure of that. Jubilee has a way of pulling you in and never letting you go."

Madeline rolled her eyes. "Yeah, people keep saying that. I'll believe it when I see it."

CHAPTER 11

*B*rady and Madeline stepped out into the cold evening, leaving the home they were sharing to go to the town's annual high school football game. From what Madeline understood, this wasn't a typical football game since the season was over. Instead, the town came together once a year to play a community football game, usually involving former players from the team at the local high school. Brady told her that anyone who had ever played on the football team could come compete in the game.

"So why aren't you playing? I thought you said you played football in high school?" Madeline asked as they drove toward the high school in Brady's truck.

"I did. I usually play every year, but last year I

hurt my knee, and I wasn't able to work the farm for a couple of weeks. I figured it wasn't worth the risk this time, especially since I'm going up and down the stairs to the basement."

"Getting old, huh?" she said, laughing.

"I guess it beats the alternative."

Madeline was excited to go to the game and get a feel for another small town event. She knew that people in the area were big football fans, so she expected it to be a spectacle. She had not been in a football stadium since her own high school years. She definitely wasn't a cheerleader back then. She was much more likely to be on the sidelines, sitting with her reading club friends.

When they got to the field, the game wasn't set to start for another thirty minutes. The festivities had started long before, however. It was almost like a carnival, the parking lot filled with people from town, food trucks, and kids running around having a good time. There were cheerleaders practicing their routines along with the high school band playing some tunes. Just hearing a high school band brought her back to her own days in school.

The field was lit with the glow of the setting sun, a huge expanse of green grass laid out before them which was set to be filled with all the town's favorite football players.

Brady led Madeline through the crowd of people, pointing out various members of the community including the mayor and the head of the county commission. He talked about the mascot, a bulldog, and some of his best memories of being a part of the team. He even found his old head football coach in the crowd and introduced Madeline. He was a large, boisterous man with a red face, and he certainly fit the profile for what Madeline thought of when she envisioned a football coach. Maybe he'd be a character in her new book.

They finally made their way to the bleachers, finding a spot that gave a great view of the field. She saw some familiar faces in the crowd, including Clemmy, who waved at her. It seemed like everybody was there. Jubilee wasn't a big place, but everybody in town seemed to be at the football game. Of course, Brady knew everybody. He waved and shook hands more times than Madeline could count. So far she hadn't seen anyone who didn't like him.

Madeline found herself getting excited about the prospect of watching the game, even though she didn't understand football at all. She remembered back in high school that her favorite part of going to the football game was sitting right behind where the players stood, watching them in their tight little football pants. She decided not to share that piece of information with Brady.

As the game kicked off, Brady started giving Madeline a running commentary, explaining the game, the players' positions, and the significance of each move. She suddenly found herself getting caught up in the game, cheering and clapping along with the crowd. She was no longer just an observer, but a part of the group, and it was exhilarating. She lost herself in it. Suddenly she wasn't thinking about her book or her home in the city. She was a part of Jubilee, and it was the most fun she'd had in a long time.

When halftime came, Brady and Madeline went over to the food trucks and enjoyed some hot dogs. They laughed and talked, their conversation easy and comfortable. Brady had lots of stories to share, and Madeline tried to file them all away in case they made good plot ideas. She was enjoying this new friendship. It had been a long time since Madeline had a new friend. And now she had Brady, Geneva and even Clemmy. How was it possible that she had just been in this place for the last few weeks, but she had made more friendships than she had in the city in just as many years?

As the game resumed, the energy in the crowd continued to be electric. Brady's enthusiasm was infectious, his loud yells and fist pumps blending in with the crowd. All the players on the field were Jubilee High School alumni, and they had been broken into two teams. Brady and Madeline were rooting for team A, for reasons she didn't understand, and when they won, half the crowd went wild. Brady stood and cheered and clapped. "Some of my best friends from my team are on that field. I guess they've still got it!"

When the game was over, they climbed into the truck and headed home. Madeline was exhausted. She hadn't expended that much energy in a long time. Her cheeks hurt from laughing, and her stomach hurt from that hotdog she ate.

"Seems like you had a good time," she said.

"I had a great time! It's always good to get together with the town, but I will use any excuse to go watch a football game."

"Thanks for taking me. That was a lot of fun. Even if I didn't know what was going on part of the time."

"You did good. I was kind of surprised."

"Surprised? Why?"

He shrugged his shoulders. "I guess I thought that you might not enjoy it."

They got out of the truck and stepped up onto the porch. Madeline suddenly felt nervous. Even though they were both going into the house, it suddenly felt like the end of a date. That moment at the front door when you wonder if he's going to kiss you, and you're either hoping he does or hoping he doesn't. She found herself hoping he would, and that was scary.

"Well, I guess we should get inside," Madeline said. The only problem was, neither of them moved. They stood at the front door, the porch light illuminating both of them.

"I guess you're right." Brady didn't move either. His voice was soft, and his gaze was fixed on her. She saw his eyes dart down at her lips. And she swore that he stepped slightly closer. Close enough that she could feel the warmth of his breath on her cheek. And just as she thought it might happen, the porch light flickered, breaking the moment. He pulled away, a slight blush coloring his cheeks.

"Good night, Brady," she said, wanting to cry. It was like a moment from one of her books, and she had never experienced one of those in real life. Only in her mind. She gave those moments to her characters, but the universe had never given her one for herself.

"Good night." He unlocked the door and walked straight to the basement, shutting it behind him. Madeline stood in the living room, and leaned against one of the log walls, letting out a long sigh. Why did life have to be so complicated?

NOW THAT BRADY was downstairs for the evening, Madeline started preparing for her next workday. She needed to get some writing done, and the most important part of that was having a nice pot of coffee in the morning. She liked to get everything ready the night before, so she set out her coffeepot, filled the tank with water, and then looked for her mug. She had an insulated mug that she could fill up and drink on throughout the morning, and the coffee stayed nice and hot. But she didn't see it anywhere. She looked all over the living room, went up into the loft, and then realized it was probably in her car. She remembered filling it with ice water the day before, after she had washed her coffee out.

"Dang it. I guess I'll just run out to my car and grab it." Madeline talked to herself all the time. She supposed it had something to do with the fact that she talked to characters in her head frequently. She unlocked the door and walked outside and went through the yard to her car. She hit the unlock button, reached in and pulled out her mug.

It was a clear night in Jubilee, a blanket of stars

above her in the sky. She would never get tired of looking at the stars and the moon. It was something she had a hard time seeing in the city because of the light pollution. All she could hear was the slight rustling of leaves, and the occasional sound of the whippoorwill far away. He typically got closer as it became time for her to go to bed.

She was working through a scene in her head as she walked back to the house, but she was stopped in her tracks by the sound of a stick breaking. Was someone there? It was completely possible that someone was hiding in the woods looking at her, and that was terrifying. Trying not to panic, she spoke.

"Is someone there? Brady? Is that you playing a trick on me?" There was no response. She knew Brady was unlikely to try to scare her, so she was confident it wasn't him. That's when she saw a silhouette. It was a large shadow, wider than a person. She walked a couple of steps closer since it was between her and the house, and when she did, her breath caught in her throat. It was the unmistakable bulky shape of a black bear, holding one of her bird feeders in his paws. He had torn off the top and was sticking his face down inside, and he seemed completely uninterested in moving on. He kept looking at her, the moonlight reflecting in his eyes.

Madeline had never been more terrified in her life. "Go! Get out of here, bear!" she yelled. The bear was undeterred. He just looked at her like she was the crazy one. "Help! Help!"

Her voice echoed through the forest, but she knew Brady would never hear her from the basement. But without any hesitation, he suddenly bolted out of the front door. She had no idea how he knew she was even out there. He closed the distance between them, standing a few feet behind the bear. Suddenly his arm raised up and the sound of an air horn pierced the night. The bear dropped the bird feeder, ran down into the backyard and disappeared.

He ran over to Madeline. "Are you okay?"

Without thinking, Madeline did something that was very UN-Madeline. She ran to him, threw her arms around his neck and hugged him tightly. "I was terrified!"

"Hey, it's okay…" Brady said, his voice so soothing. Madeline's heart pounded against her chest, and she was sure he could feel it. He rubbed her back with his hand, and she couldn't think of a time she felt safer. Realizing she was getting in too deep, Madeline stepped back and wiped a stray tear from her eye.

"I'm sorry. I know I overreacted."

"Madeline, it's normal and okay to have feelings. Emotions aren't just for your characters."

She nodded quickly. "I'll get those bird feeders out of the yard tomorrow. I didn't think they'd be attractive enough to bears, but I can see they are."

"Are you sure you're okay?" She wanted to say she wasn't nearly as scared of the bear as what she felt for him in that moment.

"I'm fine. But I am tired, so I'd better head to bed. How did you know I was out here, anyway?"

"I heard the door chime and got worried." She'd totally forgotten that the door even had a chime on it. It was connected to a security system that the owner had installed since she didn't live there full time.

They started walking toward the front door, Madeline still looking around for the bear. "You were worried about me?"

He looked over at her, his eyes soft. "Of course."

They walked inside and Madeline set her mug on the kitchen counter before making a beeline for the stairs. "Well, goodnight again."

"Goodnight, Madeline." He continued standing there while she walked up the stairs and shut her door. This was going to be one restless night of sleep.

MADELINE SAT inside the bustling coffee shop with her laptop in front of her. Sometimes she liked to work in peace and quiet, and other times she preferred to work with some white noise in the background. Coffee shops were perfect for that. She could hear conversations but couldn't really make them out. And since she knew very few people in town, nobody was going to walk up and interrupt the flow of her writing.

She had situated herself at a small table back near the fireplace. It was too warm outside for it to be turned on, and there were a couple of sofas in front of her where people would sit and chat. Today, the place was full, but she was able to fly under the radar and get her work done. She had already written five-hundred words, and she was excited about the progress of her novel.

Suddenly her phone rang, breaking her out of the flow of her writing. It was her agent, Laura. She assumed that she was going to be battering her with more questions about why Madeline let Brady move in. She definitely wasn't going to tell Laura about their almost kiss after the football game, or her slight mental breakdown after the bear sighting.

"Hello?"

"Madeline, I have big news!"

"Really? Do tell."

"There's a new publisher, and they are interested in doing a deal with you for a city series. They want something set in Manhattan."

"Wait a minute. You told me that nobody wanted my big city novels anymore, and that I should write small town. I mean, that is why I'm here in Jubilee. I'm almost two months into this, and now you're telling me that somebody wants my city books?"

"Don't be mad at me," Laura said. "This is a brand new publisher, and they just reached out a few minutes ago. They're willing to take a chance on you."

Madeline laughed under her breath. "Take a chance on me? Are you serious? I've been a heavy hitter in the romance genre for over twenty years. You make it sound like I'm a newbie."

"Okay, maybe that was a poor choice of words. But you know what I mean. They love your past work, and they're interested in this new series. That would mean that you can stop what you're working on and come back home. This could be a whole new start to your career."

"But I'm at least a third of the way through this novel. Am I supposed to just toss it in the trashcan?" Madeline couldn't believe what she was saying. Even a month ago, she would've jumped at the chance to get in her car and go straight back to her fancy lifestyle in the city. Now she was fighting to stay in Jubilee?

"I have to say, I thought you would be happier about this. I've been working myself like crazy trying to figure out a way to get you back here. Is that not what you want?"

She paused for a moment. "Of course that's what I want. But I also know I've put in a lot of work learning about this town and writing this book. It's actually going pretty well, and maybe I just want to see it through."

"Or maybe you want to stay there with sexy Brady from down the dirt road."

"That has nothing to do with it."

She knew that was a lie. Jubilee had welcomed her with open arms, and now she found herself slowly falling in love with everything about it. The simplicity of life, the charm of the people, the unity of the community, the beautiful landscape. And maybe Brady was on that list somewhere.

"I don't know what to say. This is not how I thought this call would go."

"Look, I'm not saying no. I'm just telling you that I need a week or two to make my decision."

There was a long pause on the other end of the

line. "Okay. I'll tell them that. But please promise me you're not making this decision based on Brady."

"Laura, enough. I'm a grown woman. I know what I'm doing." Did she? Did she know what she was doing? Not really.

After she hung up, Madeline stared straight ahead. There were people all over the coffee shop, but she wasn't actually looking at them. She was looking off into space, trying to figure out what to do next. Take a chance on some new publishing company that was going to publish what she already knew how to write? Or write something new and take a chance that her readers would come back? She didn't know what her choice would be, but for now she was going to keep it to herself and try to make the best decision. Whatever she decided would affect the rest of her life.

CHAPTER 12

*M*adeline was just finishing up her morning walk when she ran into Geneva near her driveway. Geneva, wearing a brightly colored red and white long dress, waved and grinned.

"Good morning!"

"Good morning, Geneva. How's it going?"

"Just been busy preparing for summer. I do a lot of our wildlife nature walks during the summer, and I've already got a full schedule of people."

Madeline marveled at how Geneva was still so active at her age. She hoped she was the same when she got into her seventies. "Won't you be hot?"

"Oh, yes. But I'm used to it. Listen, I wanted to ask you a question."

"Sure. What is it?"

"I came by to tell you about the summer kickoff festival this weekend. Every year, Jubilee residents get together on the square to celebrate the coming of summer. We have food trucks, music, activities for the kids, local vendors. That sort of thing."

Madeline thought back to the football game. "It seems like this town just thinks up reasons to eat out of food trucks."

Geneva giggled. "You're not wrong about that. Anyway, the whole town will be there, and I was hoping that you might like to participate?"

"Participate how? I don't have a food truck, and I don't sell any products."

"Well, I'd like to have a little face painting station next to my table. I'll be selling homemade jewelry and some essential oils and tinctures. While the parents are talking to me, I thought maybe you could distract the kids by painting their faces."

Madeline laughed. "I'm not exactly artistic."

Geneva waved her hand. "You don't have to be. As long as you can paint a smiley face or a balloon, you should be fine. Nobody's looking for art museum quality art here."

Feeling put on the spot, Madeline felt like she couldn't say no. Besides, she was still trying to decide what to do about the publishing contract, and this would be a nice day away from worrying about it.

"Okay, I'll do it."

Geneva's eyes widened. "You will? Oh, that's wonderful! Thank you. I'll get everything ready. You'll only need to show up."

"Well, I'd better get inside so I can practice my painting skills," Madeline said, laughing.

It was Friday, and Madeline was readying herself for the festival tomorrow. She had been practicing with paints she got at the dollar store and making little designs on copy paper. That's when she realized that she was definitely never going to be able to give up her job as a novelist to become an artist. Art didn't necessarily transfer from one medium to the other. She was good with words, but not good with paint brushes.

As she was leaving the coffee shop, she ran right into Brady on the sidewalk. He looked a little flustered at first and then smiled. "Oh, hey. I figured you were at the house."

"No, I've started doing my writing at the coffee shop a few days a week. It just gives me a little change of scenery, not that I need it. It's much more beautiful at the cabin, but the distraction of everybody talking is helpful. What are you doing in town? I thought you were at the farm."

"I needed to get some more feed for the animals."

Madeline looked at both of his hands. He wasn't carrying anything. "Did you put it in your truck?"

Brady looked down at his hands. "Oh, yeah. I guess that didn't make much sense." He chuckled. For some reason he seemed nervous, and she had never seen him that way before.

"Well, I'm going to head back to the cabin. I'm starving. I wish I had something pre-made, but I guess I'll have to start from scratch. Or maybe I'll just pick up a hamburger at the drive-through."

"I was going to head over to the tavern. Want to eat dinner together?"

"That sounds nice. I haven't checked out the tavern yet."

"It's within walking distance unless you're too tired to walk a block or two?"

"No, I definitely need my exercise. I've been sitting for hours."

Brady led her down one of the side streets and around the corner. The tavern, called The Buzzed Bear, stood out from the rest of the town. It was in a newer brick building, but it was made to look older so that it fit in with everything else. It had a bright red metal roof, and a giant bear sculpture out front.

When they walked inside, the place was buzzing with activity. Of course, it was Friday night in a small town, and there were limited things to do. Most of the stores closed up at five o'clock, even on weekends. And most places weren't open on Sundays. Madeline had found that she had better get everything she needed before Sunday, because she wasn't going to be able to find it otherwise.

The place had lots of rustic charm. It was decked out like a log cabin, with bear themed decor to create ambience. The smell of typical tavern cuisine - like chicken fingers and wings - filled the air, blending with the conversations and clinking glasses. There was a large bar made from logs, and it was full of people. Thankfully, Madeline spotted a table in the far corner where they could sit.

They took a seat, scanned the menu and then chose what they wanted to eat. Madeline got the Grizzly Burger, while Brady got the Cub salad, an obvious play on the Cobb salad. She was surprised he was ordering salad at all since most men were meat and potatoes kind of guys.

"I guess I look like a pig ordering a hamburger while you're getting a salad," Madeline said, laughing. "I'm trying to eat like the locals. Geneva said it is the only way to learn. She practically slapped me when I ordered a salad the other day at the diner."

Brady chuckled. "I normally get a burger, but I'm just feeling like I need some vegetables. I like salad, actually. And there aren't a lot of places around here that have them, or at least not good ones. This kind of town is more about barbecue and comfort food than it is about healthy eating."

"Yes, I have found that to be true. So, what did you do today?"

"I just worked at the farm. Hung out with Gilbert. Fixed a fence."

"I looked for you when I drove out, but I didn't see you anywhere. You must've been in the barn." There was just something about the way he was acting that made Madeline uncomfortable. He seemed quiet, lost in thought somewhere. Maybe it was about the house. He certainly had a lot on him trying to get his house rebuilt. He recently mentioned that he was going to get a temporary trailer and put it on the property so that he didn't have to stay with her any longer than he needed to. The thing was, she wasn't in a rush to get him out of there.

"Yeah, I was probably in the barn. So, what did you do all day?"

"Well, let's see. I did some writing, practiced my face painting…"

"How does one practice face painting?" he asked, laughing. It was good to see him loosening up a bit.

"Well, you get a piece of paper and some dollar store paints, and you practice at the kitchen table. That is until the paint goes through and gets on the table and you spend a little while cleaning that up. But, as it turns out, I am not good at art. I fear for the little children who are going to have my skills displayed on their chubby little cheeks."

He smiled. "I think it's great how you're settling into being a small-town girl."

"There are two things wrong with that statement. I'm not staying in the small town, and I'm not a girl. I wish I was, but those days have long since passed, as these newly formed crow's feet show."

"Don't talk bad about yourself, Madeline. You're one of the most attractive women I've ever seen, except the ones maybe on a movie screen somewhere, and they aren't real."

Her cheeks flushed. What was this guy doing to her? Sometimes she felt like she had landed right in the middle of her own romance novel. But it wasn't real. She was leaving. She might even be leaving sooner than she thought.

"Did y'all want something to drink from the bar?"

a young woman asked as she walked up to the table. She was wearing a green apron with an embroidered bear on the front and had her hair pulled up in a ponytail.

"I'll take the Black Bear Ale," Brady said. "It's what I always get. I recommend it."

"I'll take the same thing."

As they waited for their meals to come, the conversation flowed. Brady seemed to loosen up, and the local brew didn't hurt. Brady talked about skeet shooting and encouraged Madeline to come give it a try one day. She talked about life in the city and some of her escapades at book signings. She had all kinds of stories about interesting readers and letters she had gotten over the years, and Brady seemed to find all of that intriguing and amusing at the same time. Of course, he was getting a little buzzed on his Black Bear Ale.

When the food came, Madeline dove straight into her hamburger. It was the best one she'd ever had in her life. It was juicy and stacked high with cheese, onions, tomatoes and lettuce. It also had some kind of special barbecue sauce on it, and she felt like she looked like the world's biggest pig over there scarfing it down as quickly as possible.

Soon, they were both uncomfortably full, each of them laying back in their chairs. "I'm not even sure

I'm gonna be able to walk back to my car," Madeline said, laughing.

"That hamburger is a beast," Brady said, taking money from his wallet and laying it on the table.

"Let me pay my half," Madeline said, reaching for her purse.

"Absolutely not."

"Why? I don't expect you to pay for me."

"It's my privilege to pay for you. Besides, my mom will come straight out of that cemetery over there and smack me across the face if I let a woman pay for her own dinner. It's just not right."

"You know it's the twenty-first century, right?" Madeline said, laughing.

"It doesn't matter. Some things shouldn't change. Men should respect women, and if a man can't afford to take a woman out for dinner, then he should sit his rear end at home."

"A real southern gentleman," Madeline said, smiling. "That's a rarity."

He looked at her, his gaze focused on her face. "It shouldn't be rare, especially for a woman like you. You deserve the world, Madeline Harper. And if you don't ever fall in love with a man who will give you that, then you're better off alone. Don't settle for less."

"Why are you talking like you're not going to see me again?"

He smiled slightly. "I'll see you at home. You certainly can't get rid of me that easily. I'm just saying, when you go back to your big city lifestyle, don't settle for some loser guy who doesn't put you on a pedestal."

Her stomach was in knots. Every time they had a conversation, she found herself wanting to leap forward and press her lips to his. This was not like her at all. Maybe it was something about the mountain air.

"Well, I guess we should be going. I'm exhausted, and I can't wait to climb into my bed."

"Yeah, let's go."

When they left, the moon was high in the night sky, casting a silvery glow over Jubilee. They laughed and talked as they made their way back to their vehicles, and Madeline couldn't help but notice that Brady's presence beside her seemed to warm the cool night air. With every passing day, she was becoming a part of Jubilee, and Brady was becoming a part of her. It was dangerous territory, and it was making her decision about the publishing contract that much harder. How was she supposed to decide what to do without feelings being involved?

They finally reached their vehicles, and Madeline was grateful. She was so full from the hamburger, and her feet were killing her from walking. She just wanted to get back to the cabin and settle in for the night.

"I'll follow you home. I don't want you walking from your car to the house in the dark, just in case our bear friend is back."

"I bought an air horn, and it's in the car. I'll be fine."

He put his hand on the frame of her car door, just past her shoulder. She stood there, frozen in place wondering if he was going to finally kiss her. Instead, he leaned down and spoke. "Let me do the southern gentleman thing. We protect women around here, and if that means I need to stand between you and a bear, I'll certainly do it." He pulled on the door frame, pushing her forward into him. He smelled good. Cologne and farm work were a good mixture. She stood there for a moment, wanting to press her face into his chest, but instead she stepped sideways and then into the car. Brady closed it, smiling down at her.

"My truck is over there across the square. I'll pull behind you, and we can go."

As she watched him walk off, Madeline found herself feeling lovesick like a middle school girl. Why was this happening to her? This was the worst possible timing. Why couldn't Brady Nolan live in the city? And the answer was simple. He was part of the fabric of Jubilee, and removing him would take the Brady out of Brady. He wouldn't be who he was.

UNDER THE BRIGHT JUNE SUN, the Jubilee summer kickoff festival was in full swing. The whole town seemed to be there, and the smell of popcorn and barbecue permeated the air. There were cotton candy machines, giant inflatable jumping houses, and food trucks everywhere. There was music from local groups, and the sound of guitars and banjos seemed to come from every direction. Everyone was excited to be there, but Madeline stood behind her face painting station with her stomach fluttering while a line of eager children formed. She knew they would be disappointed later when they looked in the mirror and saw her handiwork.

"You look like you're about to get up and give a speech. Loosen up," Geneva whispered in her ear, poking her in the arm. "It's face painting, not surgery."

Madeline chuckled under her breath. "I just don't want these little kids to be sad when they look in the mirror thinking they have a butterfly on their face, but it looks like a crime scene."

"What you have to remember about festivals is that it's hot out here. These little kids are going to sweat all day long, so the face paint will be gone before they even make it home. You're just giving them a fun experience while their mothers spend a lot of money in my booth."

"You're just using me as a decoy," Madeline said, pretending to be offended. "You don't even appreciate my art." Geneva laughed loudly, causing a couple of mothers to turn around.

"Hey, Susan! I've got another color in those earrings you love so much," Geneva said, pasting on her best smile. She actually appeared to be a pretty good salesperson.

Madeline turned her attention back to the line of children and waved for a little girl to come sit down. She had perfect, almost white blonde hair going all the way down to her lower back. Her eyes were bright blue, and her skin almost the color of porcelain. Madeline had always been jealous of blondes. Her boring brown hair used to drive her crazy, but one time she had her stylist dye it blonde, and she looked ridiculous.

"Hi, my name is Madeline. What would you like me to paint for you?"

"Can you do a fairy princess wearing a pink dress and holding a magic wand?"

Madeline paused for a moment, unable to think of a way to tell the little girl that she wasn't nearly talented enough for that. "How about a heart or butterfly?"

The little girl stared at her for a moment. "A heart, I guess." Ah, the first disappointed customer of the day.

AFTER HOURS of sitting out in the heat, painting the chunky little cheeks of children in the community, Madeline was ready for a nice long nap. The festival was going for at least another two hours, so she got a large cup of lemonade and bought herself a sun hat just so she could make it.

"You can take a break if you want to," Geneva said. The older woman didn't miss a beat. She'd been handling customers like a pro all day long, only taking a break to eat lunch that she brought from home.

Madeline didn't have a line of children anymore like she'd had most of the day. She figured many of the families were getting lunch, or they had taken their kids home for a nap. Festivals were exhausting work.

She looked up to see Brady coming toward her table. "Come with me, Madeline." He had a mischievous grin on his face. "I need your help."

"What kind of help?"

"There's a community scavenger hunt, and I need you to help me win it."

"And what's in it for me?" she asked, smiling.

"The honor of helping me win a kayak."

"A kayak? Do I get half of that if we win?" she asked, standing up. She glanced over at Geneva, who was giving her a knowing smile. This whole thing was just making Geneva think that she was right about Madeline liking Brady.

"I'll take you for a ride," Brady said, laughing as he pulled on her arm. "We have to go! They're getting started."

Madeline jogged with Brady toward the center of the square where a large crowd had gathered. She had never been a part of a scavenger hunt, but it did sound fun and was certainly a welcome break from her time as a face painter.

There was an announcer with a microphone standing under a canopy. He looked like he was probably in his late sixties, and he handed out papers to each of the participants. The paper contained a list of items, and each one had a riddle to solve to figure out what the item was and where it could be found.

Brady and Madeline took their paper and quickly scanned the list. The very first riddle said "I am full of keys but can't open any door. Find me where the melodies soar." Madeline looked confused, but Brady immediately recognized it.

"That has to be the piano at the music store!" he whispered loudly into her ear before running off. She ran after him, not having any clue where the music store was. Hot on his heels, Madeline laughed as they bantered back-and-forth looking for item after item. There was a cookbook at the library, a blue flower in the park, an old baseball at the high school field. Madeline had never run around so much, and the hot Georgia sun was getting to her. She felt like a kid again, only with much older bones.

They solved every riddle and ran to the finish line, their laughter filling the town square. The very last item was a bear shaped cookie from The Buzzed Bear tavern. With all of their scavenger hunt items in their arms, they ran back to the announcer, each of them panting. By some amazing string of events, they won the scavenger hunt. Brady was so excited when they handed him the long red kayak. Each of them held one side of it and posed for a picture in the local newspaper. Madeline couldn't remember a time she'd had more fun. It was certainly different from what she would've been doing back in the city. Eating at the same old restaurants, maybe going to a bar for wine with friends.

As the last light of day faded into the twilight, the town square was aglow with the soft luminescence of countless string lights. They hung like strands of stardust, casting a magical aura around the covered pavilion. A local band was playing soft melodies, and many couples were dancing. Madeline marveled at the older couples especially, many of whom were used to being home a lot earlier than this. Still, their love kept them out there, swaying to the music in each other's arms.

Brady and Madeline stood off to the side, still reveling in their scavenger hunt win. Brady turned to her, a hint of playfulness in his eyes. "May I have this dance, Ms. Harper?" He extended his hand to her.

Madeline was caught off guard, although she shouldn't have been given that they were standing there watching other people dance. Warmth flooded her cheeks. She looked at the dance floor and then back at Brady, his eyes twinkling a bit with anticipation and his hand still extended. Despite the fact that it felt like four-hundred butterflies were having a cage fight in her stomach, she couldn't help but smile and place her hand in his.

"You may, Mr. Nolan."

Brady's hand was warm and firm, his grip secure as he pulled her out onto the dance floor. They found a spot, and he pulled her close. She could feel his heart beating against hers, and his other hand resting on the small of her back. The world felt like it shrunk down to just the two of them as their bodies moved in sync, swaying to the rhythm of the romantic music. Madeline's breath hitched when she looked up at him. His gaze was intense, yet warm and tender, and she swore she felt her heart skip a beat.

They danced with each other as if they'd done this a thousand times before. The warmth of his hand on her lower back and his fingers sending electricity down her spine felt like nothing she had ever experienced before. Sure, she had written about it a million times. But it seemed like the thing of fairytales. The scent of him, the mixture of the farm and cologne was intoxicating to her. It brought her a sense of comfort she didn't even know she had been missing all these years.

And as the music surrounded them, he pulled her closer. She could feel the heat radiating from him, and she closed her eyes, pressing her cheek to his chest, losing herself in the moment. She felt him leaning down slightly, the sensation of the stubble on his jawline against the top of her forehead.

For a moment, time stood still. Madeline had written things like that in books before, but she didn't think it was real. She felt safer in his arms than she'd ever felt in her whole life. She felt cherished and seen. The connection they had made over the past few weeks seemed to deepen in the moment, and she feared what she was going to feel when the music stopped.

When the song ended, they slowly broke apart, their eyes lingering on each other. There was an unspoken conversation going on between them. There was a shift, but there was no rush or urgency to do anything about it. With a soft smile, Brady slightly bowed toward her. "Thank you for the dance, Madeline."

She just smiled because, once again, words failed her.

CHAPTER 13

The next day, Madeline worried that things would be awkward between her and Brady. They had gone straight home from the festival, said good night and headed to their own sleeping quarters. She was surprised that he didn't try to make a move, but then she realized he might be just as freaked out as she was. After all, he knew that she was leaving in a few months, maybe sooner, if she finished her book. Maybe he didn't want to get his heart broken either. So she'd gone to sleep, had a restless night and woke up inspired to work on her book.

She had tucked away in her loft area all day, her fingers literally dancing over the keyboard as she got lost in the world she was creating. She had a surge of inspiration that finally hit her, and she planned to ride that wave as long as possible. As the hours slipped away unnoticed, she enjoyed the quiet time with her characters and just the sound of the birds outside.

In the late afternoon, it was the grumbling of her stomach that finally broke her out of her concentration. She looked at her watch in total shock. Somehow she had completely missed lunch and had been working on her book for hours. She left her computer on the desk and made her way down to the kitchen. She had no idea where Brady was today. For all she knew, he could be at the farm or have gone into town. She was too hungry to look outside to see if his truck was there.

As she pulled out the chicken and got it ready to put into the oven, she thought about how inspired she felt now. Maybe it was the dance. Maybe it was the community festival. Whatever it was, it had her juices flowing, and she felt more inspired than ever to write her book. She only had a few more days to answer about the publishing contract, but right now she was leaning toward staying with the small town book. After all, readers had spoken and said that's what they wanted. It was certainly easier to make this book a bestseller if she wrote what they wanted.

She continued gathering ingredients for the dinner she was making, and she always made sure to make enough in case Brady wanted something. But suddenly the house plunged into darkness. A storm had been brewing outside, and the power was out. She stood still for a moment, hoping it would come right back on, but it didn't. The rain drummed against the windows, and the wind howled through the trees outside. She could hear thunder in the distance and see lightning bolts dancing across the mountains.

Before she could even fumble for her phone, the soft glow of light suddenly illuminated the room. Brady was there, holding a candle in his hand. He smiled. "The power's out."

"Yeah, I can see that. Unfortunately, I got lost in my work and didn't realize I missed lunch. I was just putting the chicken in the oven for dinner, but I guess I won't be doing that."

"I think we have some leftovers in the refrigerator that we could eat. Care to have a candlelight dinner with your roommate?"

All she heard was candlelight. Sitting in a room with Brady alone during a storm in candlelight? Probably not the best thing to do, but it certainly sounded fun.

Brady walked around and lit a few more candles. Madeline had a candle addiction. She bought way more candles than she could ever use, in every scent imaginable. Back at her city home, she even had a candle cabinet that she told no one about because it was embarrassing.

Madeline opened the refrigerator, trying to get things out as quickly as possible so she could close it and preserve the cold temperature for as long as possible. With the power out, she didn't want to also lose all of her groceries.

She found some leftover chicken salad, a bowl of grapes, and got the pita bread from the kitchen counter. Brady set one of the candles in the kitchen so that she could get everything prepared. He grabbed the pitcher of tea out of the refrigerator and poured them both a glass. Before long, they were sitting at the table with their makeshift dinner, lit by the soft glow of the candles. There was just something about candlelight that totally shifted a mood no matter what you were doing.

As usual, the conversation flowed freely. They laughed and shared stories. Madeline talked about some of her fears writing a small town book, and Brady talked about his future plans for the farm. Every time they talked, it was like they got closer and closer, and Madeline felt like she was being pulled into quicksand.

Eventually, the conversation slowed, and they sat in a comfortable silence just enjoying each other's company. Madeline remembered those silent moments with her husband, but they were never comfortable. They were awkward.

She couldn't help but steal glances at Brady and watch the candlelight flicker on his face. He was handsome, and candlelight just emphasized that.

Without realizing it, Brady reached across the table and took her hand in his. It seemed to be the most natural thing in the world, and it seemed like he didn't realize he was doing it at first. The touch sent a jolt through Madeline, her heart pounding in her chest. His gaze met hers, and the room felt like it was filled with electricity. There was a question in his eyes, a silent request that she answered with a nod, her breath hitching in her throat.

He slowly stood up, never breaking eye contact with her, and stood beside her, pulling her to her feet. His hand was warm in hers, and the other hand gently cradled her face as his thumb traced her lower lip. His eyes searched hers for one last confirmation, and Madeline couldn't say no. She nodded as he leaned down, his lips meeting hers in a kiss that truly made the world stand still. It was a moment romance novels were made for, and she'd written this moment a hundred times. But no words could describe it in real life.

It was a soft, exploratory kiss as if they were discovering each other. As the kiss deepened, her heart pounded against her chest, threatening to crack her sternum wide open. His lips were soft and warm, and it felt like the first kiss she'd ever had in her life. It was everything she had imagined it would be, and yet more. When they finally broke apart, their foreheads rested against each other, she could hear the storm outside again.

"Well, that was unexpected," she said softly.

"Thank God for power outages," he responded, laughing.

MADELINE HAD NEVER SLEPT SO WELL in her life. After the power came back on, she and Brady cleaned up, said goodnight and went to their rooms. She wasn't sure if he was as freaked out as she was. All night she had the most wonderful dreams, some she could not say in proper company.

Never in her life had she felt something so powerful. Now she understood what her characters went through in her books. She was sure that Brady had gone to the farm because he had to do the early morning feeding of the animals. She put on her robe, brushed her teeth and went downstairs to find that he had already made her coffee and left her a little note.

"I'll never forget last night. Thanks for the wonderful memory. See you at dinner." He drew a little smiley face that Madeline found to be the cutest thing she'd ever seen.

She took her first sip of coffee before hearing someone knock at the front door. Silly Geneva. Why was she up this early? She walked over to the door and opened it, surprised to find her friend and agent Laura standing on her porch. She looked very out of place in her city style clothes and high heels which were a stark contrast to the peaceful back-drop of the mountains and forest. Madeline was surprised to see her standing there, and she certainly wasn't ready for a visitor this early in the morning.

"Well, are you going to let me in?" Laura asked, laughing.

"What on earth are you doing here? And so early in the morning?"

Laura brushed past her and walked into the house. "I needed to see what all the fuss was about. I can't believe I'm having a hard time getting you out of Jubilee and back to your own home. So, I drove in early this morning."

Madeline noticed that Laura had an overnight bag. "So you're planning to stay here?" That would certainly interrupt the romance she was having with Brady.

"Just for the night. It is my aunt's place. You're not happy to see me?"

Madeline smiled. "Of course I'm happy to see you," she said, hugging Laura. But she knew what this trip was about. Laura was trying to get her to come home, take the new publishing contract and break things off with Brady. But after that kiss, Madeline felt like her brain was not functioning properly. Now, all she could see was a white picket fence with her and Brady on the other side of it.

"I haven't been to this place in years. I forgot how pretty the view is," Laura said, standing in front of one of the big picture windows looking out over the Blue Ridge Mountains.

"Yes, it is beautiful."

"So, have you made any decisions about the contract?"

Madeline poured Laura a cup of coffee and slid it across the breakfast bar. "Wow, you didn't waste any time."

"There's no time to waste, Madeline. They're

waiting. This is what you wanted, so I just don't understand why there's even a question."

"Do you know how much I've written of my small town book? I'm over halfway done with it. I don't want to just throw that work away. Besides, I don't hate Jubilee as much as I thought I would, so I'm not totally in a hurry to get back to the city."

Laura stared at her, her eyes wide with surprise. "The great Madeline Harper isn't excited about going back to the city? I never thought I would hear that."

"Neither did I."

"Well, I hope you have some time to show me around today. Whenever I visited my aunt, we pretty much just stayed at the cabin. I'd like to see this town that has you so entranced."

"Okay, fine. We'll go for lunch. I'll take you to The Rustic Spoon."

"The Rustic Spoon? What kind of place is that?"

"It's our diner."

"Our?"

"You know what I mean. Let me get dressed and at least write a few words."

"Fine. I'll sit right here on this comfy sofa and return some texts."

A little while later, Madeline met Laura back

down in the living room. They walked outside and got into her car, heading for town.

"That little farm is where Brady lives," Madeline said as they drove down the road.

"That's very close. And is that where he is right now?"

"I would assume so. He's a wildlife rehabilitator and takes care of his own animals as well."

"What kind of animals?"

"Well, he has a goat named Gilbert. He's a hoot."

"Really, Madeline? You're interested in a guy who has a goat named Gilbert? Do you know how weird that sounds?"

"You seem awfully judgmental," Madeline said. "He's a good guy."

"You know nothing can happen between you two, right?"

"Right." Laura had known her for enough years to know that her response wasn't genuine.

"Oh no. Something already happened, didn't it?"

Madeline continued driving over the hills and around the curves. She hoped that she could point something out to get Laura's mind off the idea that she and Brady had already fallen for each other.

"Last night, he kissed me. We had a power outage, so we ended up eating a candlelight dinner, and one thing led to another."

"He kissed you? Oh Lord. I didn't get here in time."

"It was unreal. I've never experienced anything like that in my life."

"It was just a kiss, Madeline. People kiss each other all day long every day. It doesn't mean you have to stay in Jubilee."

"I didn't say I was staying. I'm just telling you that it was real. And it was great."

Laura laughed. "You're like a lovesick puppy. Where is the Madeline Harper I've known for all these years?"

"I'm still me. But it was a nice moment, and I'd like to bask in it for a little while longer."

They drove into the town square, and Madeline parked the car in front of The Rustic Spoon. As they got out, she noticed Laura looking around, her nose scrunching up.

"Is this it? I guess I always assumed there was more to this town that I wasn't seeing."

"This is pretty much it. We have everything we need. There's a grocery store, restaurants, gift shops, a bookstore. The hair salon is down that road. We've got the coffee shop over there." Madeline suddenly felt like she worked for the department of tourism, and she was trying to get Laura to move there.

"I don't know, I guess I just like my big stores. Where would you buy clothing?"

"We have a department store just outside of town. They sell clothes, furniture, shoes, that sort of thing."

"Interesting. Well, let's get something to eat. I'm starving."

They walked into the diner, and Madeline led Laura to a booth. The waitress walked over with her big, brown bouffant on top of her head. She wore these red cat-eye glasses with a chain on them so she didn't lose them.

"Hi, y'all. What can I get you to drink?"

Laura was staring at her like she was some sort of sideshow attraction. Madeline kicked her under the table.

"Oh, I'll just have unsweetened tea with lemon." The woman gave her a look like she was from another planet, but didn't say anything.

"Sweet tea for me."

"I'll get those ready. Here are your menus," she said, handing them the two plastic menus.

Laura flipped the menu back-and-forth in her hand like she'd never seen plastic before. "These are handy. I guess if you're accident prone, they can wipe whatever off of it."

"Are you really going to do this?"

"Do what?"

"You know what. You're the one who sent me here in the first place, but now you're coming here to poke fun at everything about this town in an effort to try to get me to go back to the city. I see through you, Laura Kearney. It's not going to work. I'm going to make the decision I want to make whether you make fun of every little thing or not."

"I'm not making fun, Madeline. I'm just pointing out that this isn't you. This isn't where you're meant to be. You have to know that. "

"You know, my whole life I have fit into the box that everybody wanted me in. Is it so bad that I'm just taking some time to learn who I am now that I am divorced?"

"I just don't want you to get stuck here."

Madeline searched her heart. She didn't feel stuck. She felt grateful. She felt blessed. She felt surprised. But she didn't feel stuck.

"Have y'all had a chance to look at the menu?" the waitress asked as she returned with their drinks.

"I'll just have a side salad," Laura said, handing her back the menu.

"I'll have a buffalo chicken sandwich with french fries," Madeline said, smiling as she handed the menu back to the server.

"You're eating a chicken sandwich? But you always order a salad."

"I'm not allowed to do that around here anymore. My friend, Geneva, will come from some other direction without me knowing it and smack it out of my hand."

Laura stared at her. "What?"

"Geneva says that I'm not allowed to eat that healthy food. I have to eat the food everybody else eats around here if I want to fit in."

"I feel like I'm living in some other dimension," Laura muttered under her breath.

"Can't you just be happy for me?"

"I'm trying. So are you saying that you're leaning toward not taking the publishing deal?"

Madeline thought for a moment. "I'm leaning toward staying in Jubilee and finishing this book."

"Ugh. That's what I was afraid you'd say."

"I'm happy here. Not to say that I won't come back home because I'm sure I will. But for now, I'm enjoying it."

"I want you to be happy, Madeline. You've been through the ringer in the last few years. I just don't want you to make a decision that's going to end up hurting you. What are the odds this thing with Brady are going to work out?"

"Laura, it's not just about that. I've met people

here that have become friends. I joined a book club. I was in a scavenger hunt, and we won a kayak."

"A kayak? Madeline Harper, who doesn't like for her nails to get chipped, is going to get in a kayak?"

"I haven't had my nails done since I got here," Madeline said, holding up her natural nails with no paint on them.

"I never thought I'd live to see the day," Laura said, laughing.

"Look, what I can say is that I have real feelings for Brady, and he has real feelings for me. And I think I owe it to myself to see this through. See what can happen. Who knows?"

"What if things do happen and you end up staying in Jubilee for good? Are you gonna be okay with that? I mean, we're talking about a tiny little town where there's nothing really to do. I don't think that's going to work for you long term."

"It might seem like there's nothing to do, but there is. There's nature. There's the book club. There are festivals all the time. It's just a different kind of lifestyle. I still love the city, but it doesn't mean I have to live there." Madeline couldn't even believe the words that were coming out of her mouth. Was she actually making the decision to stay in Jubilee permanent?

They continued chatting about this and that and

then ate their food. Madeline wanted to get back to the house so she could continue writing, and hopefully see Brady at some point. She assumed that Laura was sleeping over since she had brought a bag with her, and introducing her to Brady was already making her nervous.

They finished lunch and walked back out onto the square. Madeline offered to walk around and show Laura some of the shops. If there was one thing Laura liked to do, it was shop. Maybe that would make her think differently of Jubilee.

First, they went into the small gift shop closest to the diner. Laura picked up a candle and some chocolates. They went to the next store which was mostly T-shirts, but Laura wasn't interested in that at all. Madeline suggested that they go get a cup of coffee, so they started walking toward the coffee shop.

"I see Brady right down there," Madeline said, pointing at one of the side roads that ran off of the square.

"Oh, he's cute."

"Let's walk over there, and I'll introduce you," Madeline said, turning to go down the road. But before they could get any closer, her heart stopped. Brady was with a woman. She wasn't much younger than him, it appeared, and she was beautiful. She had long brown hair, a petite figure, and he was hugging her. Tightly. After they finished hugging, they put their arms around each other and continued walking the other direction. Madeline wanted to throw up. Here she had thought they were forming a bond, and he was apparently doing the same thing with some other woman in town.

"Oh, Madeline. I'm so sorry."

"Are you, though?" Madeline said, turning and walking toward her car.

"Yes, I am. I don't want you to be upset. Especially after what happened with Jacob."

Madeline made it to her car and unlocked the door, sitting inside and staring straight ahead. She felt like the wind had been completely knocked out of her. This is what she deserved for trusting another man. This is why fictional boyfriends were much better than real ones.

"I can't believe it. I didn't think he was that kind of guy."

"Well, unfortunately those kinds of guys live everywhere, even in small mountain towns."

"I'll take the publishing deal."

"Are you sure?"

"Yes."

Madeline knew she was making a rash decision. She knew it was immature. She knew she should stay there and finish what she started. But none of that mattered. Brady had been lying to her and was obviously involved with another woman. She wasn't going to stay there and make a fool of herself. She would go back to the city. Go back to what she knew. Go back to living a life where she lived vicariously through the characters she created. It was much safer. After all, your heart couldn't be broken when none of it was real.

CHAPTER 14

*L*aura had offered to stay the night, but Madeline asked her to go back home. She wanted to deal with this situation with Brady on her own, and she was tired of being embarrassed. Laura had now watched her be cheated on by two totally different men. It was demoralizing.

After getting back to the cabin, she tried to write some words. But all of them came across as angry. She decided that writing a romance novel when she was angry was probably not the best thing to do. Besides, she didn't need the book anymore. She was going back to her city books with a new publisher, and she was leaving this experience in the past.

As she stood in the living room looking at the table, the place where they had eaten by candlelight, her stomach turned. She couldn't believe she was so silly. At fifty-five years old, she couldn't walk around like a lovesick schoolgirl. One kiss almost made her make a terrible life decision. What did that say about her? Was she really that needy?

As she had suspected, she didn't need anybody, especially a man. She would go back to living the life of Madeline Harper, the famous author. Jubilee would just be a distant memory. And she was fine with that, or at least that's what she was telling herself.

She walked into the kitchen and got a glass of water. Just as she was taking the first sip, she heard the front door open. Brady. He was home earlier than normal.

"Hey. How has your day been so far?" he asked, standing at the edge of the kitchen, smiling. She wanted to slap the smile right off his face.

"About the same as always." She turned and poured out the rest of the water before walking past him to go upstairs.

"Listen, I don't want to interrupt your work day. I know it's important that you get your writing done. But I was hoping to take you out on an official date tonight. I thought maybe we could try that new steakhouse."

"Thanks for the offer, but I'm kind of busy right now."

He paused for a moment, looking confused. "Okay then. Maybe tomorrow night?"

"I'm actually going to be busy then, as well. I have to pack my things."

She started walking up the stairs, but she heard Brady's footsteps quickly following her.

"Madeline, what are you talking about? You're going to be here at least another three or four months, right?"

"Actually, things changed. I was offered a new publishing contract, so I'll be going home. Immediately." Without another word, she marched up the stairs and shut her bedroom door. But Brady wasn't done. She heard him coming up the stairs right after her.

"Madeline, open the door. What's going on?" he asked, tapping on her door. She wanted to ignore him, but she knew he was stubborn like she was, and he wasn't going to go away.

She opened the door and looked at him. He looked so sad, but she couldn't allow that to get to her. This was the same guy that was hugging a woman and putting his arm around her just a little bit ago. The same guy who was kissing her last night.

"It just isn't going to work out, Brady. I enjoyed our time getting to know each other, but this publishing deal is too good to pass up. I wish you the very best in your life."

"I can't believe you're saying this. Did I do something wrong?"

She paused for a long moment. "No. I just need to make the right choice for myself," she said, forcing herself not to cry. The look on his face was one of devastation. He looked more distraught right now than he did when his house burned down right in front of him. She just couldn't make sense of why he would be with another woman, and she certainly wasn't going to lower herself to asking him about it.

"I thought we had something special between us. I'm very sorry to see that you didn't feel the same way."

"Goodbye, Brady." She shut the door, burst into tears and slid down onto the floor, her head in her hands. How had everything changed so quickly? One thing was for sure. Romance novels aren't real.

FOR THE NEXT couple of days, Madeline avoided Brady as much as possible. He didn't seem to be interested in seeing her either. She didn't know where he was, and she didn't care. The more she thought about all of it, the angrier she got.

Why did he do that to her? Why did he get her feelings involved, kissed her, danced with her? All for nothing? All so he could have two women?

She just needed to focus on getting back home. She was almost finished packing everything, and she had said her goodbyes to Clemmy at bookclub last night. Now it was time to say goodbye to Geneva.

She knew that Geneva was going to have questions, and Madeline didn't plan on answering them. She didn't want Geneva to try to mediate between her and Brady. She just wanted to go home.

As she stood at the big window overlooking the mountains, there was a part of her that knew she would miss this place. How could she not? It was one of the most beautiful places she had ever visited, and she'd been all over the world.

She didn't want to admit it to herself, but she was going to grieve the loss of Jubilee. The loss of the new life she had been building with new friends. Madeline was able to be more of herself in Jubilee than she had ever been anywhere else. She just didn't realize it at first.

And now Brady had stolen that away from her. He'd made her feel like she was falling in love with him, and then let her see that it was all a lie. He didn't even know it. He had no idea that she had seen him. But Madeline did not like to be made to look a fool. She wasn't going to play the part of the jilted woman. She was just going to leave town and get back to her previous life.

Madeline walked down the road towards Geneva's house. She wanted to get this over with. She knocked on the front door, and Geneva opened it, a big smile on her face.

"Did you smell it?"

"What?" Madeline asked, confused.

"I made my famous vegetable and potato stew. I figured you might've smelled it and came over to get some."

Madeline shook her head. "No. I'm sure it's wonderful, but that's not why I'm here. I came to say goodbye."

Geneva's eyes widened. "What? You're not supposed to leave for a couple of more months at least. What happened?"

"My agent called me. A new publisher is willing to give me a contract for the same kind of books I've always written. So I'm going back."

"You know that's the wrong decision, Madeline. What about Brady?"

Madeline wanted to scream. She wanted to tell Geneva that Brady had another woman on the side that nobody probably even knew about. Instead, she just smiled slightly. "I always told you that wouldn't work out. You've been reading too many romance novels."

Geneva chuckled. "Are you sure I can't talk you out of it?"

"I'm sure. But I did want to thank you for welcoming me here and helping me so much. I know I wasn't the easiest person to befriend when I first got here, but you never gave up. So, thank you."

"You're very welcome," Geneva said, pulling her into a tight hug. "I'm going to miss you. You're a good lady, Madeline Harper. Don't ever let anyone tell you otherwise."

"Thank you." Tears threatened to stream down Madeline's face, but she willed them to stay in her eyes. She felt like she was giving up the life she never knew she wanted, but now wanted desperately.

"Travel safe," Geneva said.

"I will. And I'll call you. I will never forget you, Geneva Whitby."

"And I'll never forget you, Madeline Harper." Before she could burst into tears right in front of her friend, Madeline turned and walked quickly back to the house.

MADELINE PUT the last of her bags in her car. She turned to look at the cabin, her eyes watering. It would be weird not to wake up to the sound of the crows in the morning. It would be strange not to hear the whippoorwill at night, lulling her to sleep. And it would be strange not to look out her window and see the blue tinged mountains stretching as far as her eyes could see.

But this was the right decision. At least that's what she kept telling herself.

She thought several times about telling Brady what she'd seen, hoping that there was a reasonable explanation. But no matter how many times she rolled it around in her head, she couldn't think of one. The love he had for the woman she saw him with was undeniable. It wasn't a friend. It wasn't an acquaintance. It was someone he knew well enough to hold in his arms like that.

She had talked to Laura that morning and told her she was coming home. Laura's aunt spoke to Brady directly and told him he was welcome to stay in the house until his trailer came. Apparently, he had let her know the trailer was arriving later in the week, and he would be moving out.

Madeline and Brady had managed to avoid each other for days, and she wasn't even sure he was staying at the house anymore. For all she knew, he could be living in the barn.

And then there was Gilbert. She was sad that she didn't get to say goodbye to him. That goofy little goat had really worked his way into her heart.

There were so many things she was going to miss about Jubilee. Her favorite coffee drink. Going to book club. Hearing the bells ring every half hour from the courthouse. Little things and big things, she would miss them all. And that alone was surprising to her. The Madeline who had arrived in town just a couple of months ago would've never believed it.

She got into her car and started driving down the road, unwilling to look at the house in her rearview mirror. A person can only take so much. But she couldn't help but look at Brady's farm down at the end of the road. She could see him off in the distance feeding the horses, and her heart squeezed in her chest. Should she stop and say a formal goodbye? Should she scream an obscenity out the window and take off in a blaze of glory? That last one was a little more dramatic, and definitely not something she'd ever do.

Instead, she drove away. She didn't look back. She was going home today, only she wasn't really sure where home was anymore.

THREE WEEKS Later

Madeline sat at her desk and stared out over the gardens in her yard. She liked to tell people that she planted them herself, but the reality was that her gardener did it. She did very little around her home, including cleaning it. Now it felt weird. It felt like she should go out there and get her hands dirty, or maybe look to buy a goat.

The last three weeks back in the city had been challenging, to say the least. After she got home, she met with her new publishers. She didn't really like them very much. The kind of series they wanted her to write didn't feel authentic to her anymore, and now she didn't really know where she fit in. In fact, she had continued writing on her small town book, which was weird because she was never going to be able to publish it. She just couldn't leave those characters behind, their story unfinished.

She felt pulled in both directions. She wanted to be a successful author, but she wanted to be in Jubilee. Those two things didn't seem to go with each other.

Laura had encouraged her to sign the contract with the new publishers, but for some reason Madeline had waited. They were getting antsy and irritated. They wanted to put out some social media posts and a press release that they had finally landed the great Madeline Harper. She had promised to come sign the contract tomorrow, but her stomach was in knots about it. Something about the whole deal just didn't feel right to her, even though the advance money was great.

Just as she was trying to get back to writing her new book, the doorbell rang. Madeline wasn't expecting anyone, which did remind her of Geneva. She would always show up at the most inopportune moments. She missed that woman.

When she opened the door and saw Geneva standing there, she thought she was having a hallucination.

"Geneva?"

Geneva smiled and laughed loudly, pulling her into a hug. "I bet you're surprised to see me!"

"I'm very surprised. How did you even know where I live?"

"I'm pretty good on the Internet. Are you going to invite me in?"

"Of course. Come on in. What are you doing in Atlanta?"

"Oh, my doctor wanted to send me to a specialist. I'm having some problems with my hip. I might need surgery."

"Oh no. How would you take care of yourself alone?"

"I'd have to go to a rehab center. Doesn't that sound terrible? Stuck with a bunch of old people for weeks on end?"

"Well, no matter what, I'm glad to see you. How's everything back in Jubilee?"

"About the same. Except for that poor Brady. He just has so much on his plate."

Madeline imagined he was planning a wedding or something like that. Her mind tended to go to the worst-case scenario.

"Oh?"

"Well, he got his trailer, so that's where he's living now. He's trying to find a contractor to rebuild the house, so that's a stress."

"Well, at least he has help from his girlfriend."

"Girlfriend? What on earth are you talking about?"

"Geneva, you don't have to cover for him. I saw him right before I left. I was coming out of the diner going to the coffee shop, and I saw him with a woman. He was hugging her, and he had his arm around her. It was obvious he loved her."

"Oh dear. What did she look like?"

"She had long brown hair. Petite."

"Madeline, you misunderstood."

"How could I misunderstand that? We had started really falling for each other, and then I see him with another woman. I wasn't going to stay in town and look like a fool."

"I fear you're going to look like a fool anyway, my dear."

"What do you mean?"

"That was his sister. Jasmine."

"What? Brady told me his sister was gone. I assumed he meant she died."

"She's very much alive, Madeline. She's five years younger than him."

"Then why did he never tell me that?"

"Jasmine has had a challenging life. She's made a lot of poor decisions over the years, and for a long time she and Brady didn't have a relationship. He didn't like to talk about it, so he never mentioned her to people."

"Then why was he hugging her?"

"A few weeks ago, Brady got a call. Jasmine was in trouble. She had been married to a man that was abusing her, and of course Brady never knew it. He would've hunted him down and killed him if he had known. He helped Jasmine get into a safe house for abused women. When you saw them on the street, that was the first time he was able to touch her. Her husband had beat her up, and the police finally caught him. He's in jail now. So what you saw was Brady hugging his sister after many years. He was hugging her because she was finally free and safe."

Madeline felt like she was going to throw up. There was no way she could've known the truth about Jasmine, of course, but now she felt terrible for having treated him the way she had. Instead of being mature and asking him about what she had seen, she had assumed the worst. Most likely she had jumped to that conclusion because of what Jacob had done. She now realized that she had unfairly convicted Brady of it, too.

"I don't believe this. I threw away a perfectly wonderful relationship because I didn't understand what I saw."

"He didn't want to tell you what was going on with his sister because he didn't want to burden anybody else with it. Now she and her little girl are living on his farm, and he's trying to take care of all of them. And he's heartbroken."

"Heartbroken?"

"Madeline, he loved you. He told me so. He doesn't understand why you left."

"I have to go back. I'm miserable without him. I'm miserable without Jubilee."

Geneva's eyes watered, and she held her hands in a prayer position under her chin. "I can't believe what I'm hearing! The Madeline I met didn't want to be in Jubilee any longer than she had to, and now here you say that you're miserable without it."

"Well, you and Brady both told me that once Jubilee gets a hold of you, you can't get free. I finally understand what that means."

"What are you going to do now?"

"I'm going to pack my things."

CHAPTER 15

*I*t was a hot day in Jubilee. Madeline parked her car in the driveway of the cabin and got out, sweat beading on her forehead. It had been a long drive from Atlanta, and she had called Laura on the way to tell her to ask her aunt if she could stay at the house again. In fact, she wanted to stay there for an extended period. Laura, realizing that Madeline had changed a lot, agreed to call her aunt and ask. Thankfully, she said that was fine.

Madeline also told Laura that she was not going to sign the new publishing deal. Although, as her agent, she was a little bummed out about it, as her friend she understood. She had watched Madeline struggle back in the city, wanting to be back in Jubilee, wishing her relationship with Brady had worked out.

And now, here she was, just a few hundred feet from his farm. She hopped on the golf cart and started driving that direction. She didn't know what his reaction would be. For all she knew, he didn't want anything to do with her. After all, she abandoned him in his time of need, even though she didn't know that at the time.

She got to the end of the road and pulled the golf cart over before jumping out and walking through the woods towards his house. She saw his truck parked, so she knew he was home. She walked to the door of the barn and called his name, but she got no response except for Gilbert who came running, making his funny noises and trying to lick her leg.

She walked through the barn to the other side where she saw Brady using the water hose to fill the trough. He didn't see her yet. She watched him for a few moments, taking in the sight of him. Knowing that he hadn't done anything wrong made her want to run and give him a hug.

He turned off the hose, wound it up and then turned around. His eyes met hers. His face didn't change. There was no smile. There was no hint that he was happy to see her.

"What are you doing here?" His voice was monotone, like there was no emotion at all behind it. He wasn't happy to see her, that much was obvious.

"I didn't know."

"You didn't know what?" A hint of irritation wrapped around his words.

"When my friend Laura was here visiting, we went to town to eat at the diner. This was the day after we kissed. I saw you with a woman. I thought you were seeing somebody else. It triggered me, and that's why I left."

"That was my sister. Why didn't you just ask me? Haven't I proved to you that I'm trustworthy?"

"My husband cheated on me. And I didn't know it bothered me so much until I saw you on the street. I couldn't make sense of what I was looking at. I'm sorry that I hurt you."

"And so you thought you could just come back here and say you're sorry and everything would go back to normal? You're the first woman I've opened my heart to in many years, and you couldn't even trust me enough to ask me about what you saw." He walked past her into the barn, out of the harsh sunlight. She turned and followed him.

"I'm so sorry. It was immature for me not to talk to you about it. You didn't deserve my reaction."

"No, I didn't. At least we agree there."

"I don't know what to say, Brady. I came back because I love Jubilee. And whether things work out with us or not, I'm staying here. I went home, and I realized that the city wasn't where I needed to be. This is my home now."

He walked closer. "This is your home?"

"Yes. These mountains reeled me in, just like you said they would."

His face softened. "So, you're not going back to the city at all?"

"Nope. I'm here for good. I'm hoping I can talk Laura's aunt Dahlia into letting me buy that house, but if not I'll just buy another one."

He smiled slightly. "And you haven't been drinking?"

"No, sir. This is all me. Madeline Harper, Jubilee resident."

"My life is complicated right now. You know that?"

"I've heard. Geneva came to see me in the city."

"My sister and my niece live here now. They're out doing some grocery shopping."

"I would love to meet them. That is, if you would let me."

"I'd like to ask you a question."

"Okay, shoot."

"Would you go out on an official date with me, Madeline?"

"Nothing would make me happier."

He closed the distance between them, pushing

her against the wall of the barn and pressing his lips to hers. In that moment, Madeline Harper knew exactly where she was meant to be. Home wasn't just Jubilee. Home was wherever Brady Nolan was.

CHECK out all of Rachel's books at www. RachelHannaAuthor.com.

·

Made in United States
Troutdale, OR
09/11/2023

12802129R00148